THE GIRL WITH THE PERSIAN SHAWL

Elizabeth Mansfield

JOVE BOOKS, NEW YORK

This is a work of fiction. Names, characters, places, and incidents either are the product of the author's imagination or are used fictitiously, and any resemblance to actual persons, living or dead, business establishments, events, or locales is entirely coincidental.

THE GIRL WITH THE PERSIAN SHAWL

A Jove Book / published by arrangement with the author

PRINTING HISTORY
Jove edition / December 2002

Copyright © 2002 by Paula Schwartz
Cover design by George Long
Cover photo by Wendi Schneider

Visit our website at
www.penguinputnam.com

ISBN: 0-515-13414-7

A JOVE BOOK®
Jove Books are published by The Berkley Publishing Group, a division of Penguin Putnam Inc., 375 Hudson Street, New York, New York 10014.
JOVE and the "J" design are trademarks belonging to Penguin Putnam Inc.

PRINTED IN THE UNITED STATES OF AMERICA

10 9 8 7 6 5 4 3 2 1

ONE

꧁꧂

Mr. Josiah Crowell heaved a huge sigh. Although his position as business advisor of the Rendell estate made it inappropriate for him to display his emotions, this time he couldn't help it. Miss Kate was disputing his advice. Again.

He pushed his spectacles lower down on his nose and peered over them to examine his client more closely. *What's the matter with the girl?* he asked himself in annoyance.

Yet it had all started out so well. The drive from London yesterday, his companion on the journey, the night spent at the inn in Ipswitch, and even the weather—they'd all been extraordinarily pleasant. He'd arrived here at Rendell Hall this morning in the highest spirits. He'd convinced himself that there would be no difficulty with Miss Kate Rendell this time, for most of the matters that brought him were trivial. But here he was, right in the middle of a bumble-bath.

She stood across the room from the library table where he sat, her pointed chin tilted upward, her lips pressed tightly together, and her arms crossed over her chest in a stance that spoke loudly of her opposition. Perhaps he should have anticipated this difficulty. Kate Rendell was nothing if not decided. And when she made up her mind, there was little anyone could do to change it.

Her appearance was certainly appealing (soft, brown hair now carelessly piled atop her head, perfect oval face, patrician nose, and dark-brown eyes that seemed to hold secrets a man immediately yearned to unlock), so appealing, in fact, that Mr. Crowell did not like to think of her as stubborn. At this moment, however, he felt that no other word would do. Her father, the late Viscount, had never been headstrong, and her mother, Lady Isabel Rendell (who was at this moment sitting near the fire on the far side of the room, calmly stitching away at her embroidery), was always pleasant and agreeable. Yet—there was no doubt of it—their daughter was stubborn. Stubborn to the point of obstinacy.

He wondered, as he'd often done before, if that "decidedness" was the reason she was still unwed at the age of twenty-four. Stubbornness was not a quality that men found endearing. He himself thought her quite irksome when she grew obstinate, even though he was very fond of her at other times. And obstinate she was at this moment. After all, what he'd asked of her was not so very difficult. He only wanted her to *speak* to Lord Ainsworth, not necessarily to accede to his request.

Lady Isabel, as if she'd read his mind, spoke up at that moment. "I don't wish to interfere, Kate, my love, for you are the arbiter of our affairs, not I, but it does seem to me that Mr. Crowell is not asking so very much of you."

"Not asking *much* of me?" The tall young woman swung about and threw her mother an irritated glare. "How can you say that? He brought the interloper right into our home without so much as a by-your-leave!"

Josiah Crowell sighed again. "There wasn't time to inform you, Miss Kate. His lordship's letter reached my desk only two days ago. In it, he explained that he would be free to come to Suffolk only these two days. And since I had already planned to come out from London also, it seemed convenient—"

Kate Rendell stopped him with a wave of her hand. "Did it not strike you as an utterly ridiculous request, as well as a presumptuous one?"

"It did not seem so to me." He looked at her over his spectacles, his eyes pleading. "If I may be permitted read his letter to you . . . ?"

Kate was about to cut him off again, but his helpless expression kept her from doing it. Mr. Crowell had been the business agent for the family for fifty years, and her father had been quite right when he spoke of him as both sensible and loyal. The agent did not deserve to be ill-treated. "Very well, read it if you must," she said grudgingly and threw herself into the nearest chair.

Mr. Crowell sifted through the papers in front of him and pulled out the document in question. " *'My dear Mr. Crowell,'* " he read aloud, " *'I am writing to you in regard to a painting for which I have been searching for several years. Though unsigned, it was painted more than one hundred years ago by my grandfather, John Gerard, Earl of Ainsworth, who was considered a gifted artist. The painting disappeared from our estate during the upheaval caused by the Young Pretender's march south from Scotland in 1745. My agents inform me that a painting, called* Girl with Persian Shawl, *owned by the estate of the Viscount Rendell, seems to match the description of the missing Ainsworth work. I would very much appreciate your obtaining permission for me to call at Rendell Hall to see the painting sometime this week, when I plan to be in town.'* "

Crowell removed his spectacles and rubbed his nose. "The gentleman adds in a post script," he said, keeping a wary eye on his client, "that, should your painting turn out to be the missing work, he is willing to recompense you in the sum of 500 pounds."

"Indeed!" Kate responded in a voice of ice. "How good of him!"

"It is, I believe, a more than generous offer for an unknown artist's work. A very generous offer, I assure you. Why, I've heard of a Rowlandson that went for half that price."

Kate rose from her chair in slow dignity, like an

offended goddess. "I have no interest in the gentle-man's 'generosity.' The painting is not for sale. The very suggestion that it does not belong to us—that it may have been acquired by dealings with looters or smugglers—is insulting!"

"But my dear," murmured her mother, pausing to wet the end of a piece of yarn with her tongue and thread her needle, "it didn't seem to me that the letter accuses us of having acquired the painting illegally."

"The suggestion is implicit in his reference to his painting's 'disappearance' in the upheaval of war. Let's make short work of this, Mr. Crowell. Go and tell the man to take himself off."

Crowell fingered his neckcloth nervously. "Would you not consider telling him yourself, my dear? He seemed very sure that his informants had found the right artwork. I don't think I can be as convincing as you in dismissing his reasoning."

"Good God, man, you needn't reason with him at all!" Kate snapped. "Just tell him to go!"

"But he's come all the way from London—"

"I don't care if he's come from Timbuktu! I won't—"

"Come now, Kate," scolded her mother mildly, "I see no reason for you to raise a dust. The poor man has been cooling his heels in the drawing room for half an hour, and none of us has even thought to offer him so much as a cup of tea. You know that I dislike to interfere with your decisions, but, really, *someone* must go to him."

Kate's imperious posture wilted. Her mother's gentle reprimand made her ashamed of her own short temper. "You're right, Mama," she said with a defeated sigh. "Very well, I'll see to him. But in future, Mr. Crowell," she added on her way to the door, "I hope you'll refrain from inviting visitors to our premises whose object is to denude us of our precious artifacts."

As she strode down the hall to the drawing room, Kate seethed. Lord Ainsworth, she thought, must be a crafty old codger to have arranged a visit like this without warning. He probably knew that what he was asking was worse than presumptuous! What business had he to question the rightful ownership of anything under this roof?

On the threshold of the drawing room, she paused to calm herself and, without making her presence known, eyed the man who stood in the center of the room, his back to her. The tilt of his head and the manner in which his hands were clasped behind his back suggested that he was completely absorbed in studying the painting over the fireplace. Kate took a moment to study it, too.

She'd never really liked the work, despite the fact that the family had always considered it the finest painting in their collection. It was a portrait of a great-great-aunt, Kate had been told. The girl in the painting was undoubtedly beautiful, and the shawl that was draped from her left shoulder to hang in luxurious splendor over her right arm—a heavy but lustrous dark-blue twilled silk, with imaginatively ornate silver, green, and rust-colored leaves subtly interwoven throughout—made a dramatic contrast to the soft white gown she was wearing. It was undeniably a magnificent painting. But Kate had always been put off by the look of arrogance in the girl herself. Something about the haughty tilt of her head, the supercilious expression of her mouth, and the dark, hooded eyes looking out at her viewers with a sidelong glance, as if she were challenging their right to stare at her— all this made Kate dislike her. Nevertheless, she would never consider giving up the painting. It was a family treasure, and so it would remain. "She is quite lovely, isn't she?" she asked aloud.

"Yes, very," the man said without turning. "Except for—" Then, shaking himself from his reverie, he turned round.

The first sight of him startled her. Lord Ainsworth was younger than she'd imagined, certainly not past thirty, startlingly light-eyed, and—though she was reluctant to admit it—quite prepossessing in spite of his dark hair slightly receding from his forehead. "Except for what?" she couldn't resist asking.

"Except for a certain arrogance in her expression." He took a step toward her and smiled. "Miss Rendell, I take it?" he asked as he made his bow. "How do you do, ma'am? I'm Harry Gerard."

"Lord Ainsworth," she said with strict formality, returning his bow but not offering her hand.

Aware of the slight, his own smile faded, "I hope my observation about the girl in the shawl didn't offend you."

"No, it didn't. I expected it of you."

"Expected it?"

"Yes. It is good strategy, is it not, to belittle a work which you really desire to purchase?"

It was an offensive remark, but the only indication Lord Ainsworth gave of taking offense was a slight lift to his left eyebrow. "I don't belittle it at all," he said gently. "The girl's expression in no way detracts from the superb artistry of the work." He turned again to the painting. "I'm sorry that it isn't—"

"For sale? And so you should be, for I will never part with it."

He heard the ice in her voice and looked back at her, the left eyebrow rising higher. "Excuse me, Miss Rendell, but you needn't—"

"I must say, my lord," she cut in with an impatient toss of her head, "that I don't understand the cause of your visit here. In fact, I cannot imagine how you came to have any information about this painting at all. I can only assume that your agents bribed one of my staff to give them details of the possessions in this house."

"Not so, I assure you," the gentleman said, the tone of his denial not only lacking in hostility but actually pleasant. "The painting is listed in the *Compendium Pictorial,* you see, and the description there, though admittedly inadequate, made me believe—"

"Be that as it may," Kate interrupted impatiently, "there is no question at all that the work belongs to the Rendell estate. Though it is unsigned, there is evidence that it was painted early last century by Sir Anthony Van Dyke when he came to England."

"I don't doubt—"

"I assume you will argue that a painter of Van Dyke's acclaim would not be so remiss as to leave a work unsigned, and that, therefore, nothing on the painting can attest to its origins—"

"Miss Rendell, I make no such—"

"—nevertheless," Kate went on as if he hadn't spoken, "there is good and sufficient evidence in the family records to prove its origin."

"Miss Rendell, I have not the slightest—"

"The household accounts of the year 1625," she proceeded grandly, "show a payment of ninety pounds for a portrait of my great-great-aunt, Matilda Rendell Quigley, to a certain A.V.D."

"I'm quite sure you're—"

"And even the most suspicious connoisseur would agree that the confluence of the year Van Dyke was painting portraits in this country with the initials in the records is proof enough even to convince a court of law."

"My dear lady, a lawsuit was never *consid*—"

"As far as I'm concerned, however, it doesn't matter *who* painted the portrait, or *when*. It has hung here in this drawing room all my life. I'm accustomed to seeing it there. I would not part with it if I were offered ten times the amount you mentioned in your letter."

"But I—"

"Don't even *think* of offering more, my lord! I would not part with it for any—"

"Miss Rendell, *enough!*" The gentleman, laughing, put up his hands as if to protect himself from further onslaught. "Let me insert a word, *please!*"

Kate, startled by so unaccustomed an interruption, could only gasp, "What—?"

"I've been *trying* to tell you that you needn't prove *anything* to me. This is *not* the painting I've been looking for."

She blinked in astonishment. "It is *not*—?"

"No. My great-grandfather's style of painting was, I suspect, not nearly so skilled. The painting I'm looking for is probably softer, with less contrast between light and shadow. And the subject, I'm told, is fair-haired, not dark. I saw at once that this is not the right painting. I waited only to apologize to you for my intrusion. Now that I've done so, I have only to thank you and take my leave." He bowed and walked swiftly to the door.

Kate, realizing with a shock that she'd let loose a tirade over nothing, felt her cheeks grow hot in humiliation. She'd made an utter fool of herself!

At the door, he turned back to face her again. "I only wish to add, ma'am," he said, an unmistakable gleam of amusement in his eyes, "that even if I'd had any doubts of the ownership of that painting, seeing you would have dispelled them. The face of the girl in the shawl shows a *remarkable* resemblance to your own. Good day, ma'am." And he was gone.

Kate gaped after him, her emotions in a turmoil. Why, the dastard had insulted her! He as good as called her arrogant! *'The face shows a remarkable resemblance to your own,'* indeed! That blasted bounder! And then he'd run off like a craven, without waiting a moment for her reply. It was infuriating! She wished more than anything to have come back at him with a sharp rejoinder.

Especially if she could have thought of one.

TWO

Percival Greenway, Esquire, was down on one knee again.

Kate eyed him with barely concealed impatience. She was sorry she'd permitted the butler to admit him. It was bad enough to have to make conversation with him while seated opposite the *Girl with Persian Shawl* (the painting that she'd barely noticed all these years but that had suddenly become a source of irritation to her), but to have to endure another of Percy's offers was the outside of enough. No matter how firmly she'd expressed her refusal of his two earlier declarations, Percy seemed unable to take her seriously.

She rose from the sofa. "Please, Percy, not again," she said, turning away from him.

"Can't you allow me to finish?" Percy demanded as he stumbled to his feet.

"No!"

Percy, apparently unperturbed, responded merely by bending over and brushing the dust from the knee of his britches. The meticulous care with which he did it filled Kate with disgust. Why, the mawworm was showing more concern for his britches than for her response!

She stalked across the room to the window. Outside, a heavy rain was pelting down, blurring her view of the woods beyond the lawn. Only this morning, before the ordeal with Lord Ainsworth, she'd gazed out of these windows upon a very different scene. The autumn landscape had delighted her eyes. The rays of the morning sun, slanting through the trees, had painted the misty air with golden streaks and given the dying leaves a russet glow. But all too soon, the clouds had thickened, darkening the sky much as the visit of Lord Ainsworth had darkened her mood. Then the rain, making a curtain of tears that muddied the colors of the landscape, had turned the gold-and-russet leaves—and her spirit—to a lackluster brown. *Blast Ainsworth*, she thought, *and blast this rain!*

To make matters worse, with the rain had come the persistent Percy Greenway. Now she had to put up with another awkward interview—a repetition of his tedious marriage offers. It was the last straw!

Percy came up behind her. "I've written a poem this time," he said, putting a hand on her shoulder. "Perhaps the wording will make my addresses more appealing."

She turned and faced him, impatience battling with pity within her. She had no wish to cause him pain.

He was an old friend, after all. His family estate marched with hers on the north border. They'd been playmates through all their childhood. She, having no brothers or sisters, had been grateful to have him as a companion. But after he'd gone off to school and then to Cambridge (from which he'd been sent down after only a year), he'd returned a different fellow—more shallow and trivial than she remembered. Though tall and fairly presentable in appearance, he'd turned into a veritable fop. The high points of his collar, the shocking colors of his waistcoat, the overabundant curls of his hair were absurd enough to dismay her, but his conversation was worse. It was filled with the latest on-dits and gossip of the London ton, proving what a fribble he'd become. She took no pleasure in his company these days. But he seemed not to notice the change in her attitude toward him. *How,* she wondered, *can I make him understand?*

She shook his hand from her shoulder. "Putting the wording into rhyme will make not the slightest difference," she told him bluntly.

He stepped back, offended. "How can you tell if you haven't heard—?"

Kate, weakening at his hurt expression, shrugged in resignation. "Oh, very well," she murmured, "go ahead, if you must. But I assure you my answer will be the same."

Percy brightened, took her by the hand, and led her back to the sofa. Then he drew in a deep breath, clutched his hands to his breast, and began to declaim:

> *"My love is of a birth as rare*
> *As is for object strange and high;*
> *It was begotten by despair—"*

Her burst of laughter cut him off. *"Upon impossibility,"* she concluded for him.

"Oh, damnation!" he cried in chagrin, sinking down on the sofa and dropping his head in his hands. "You knew it!"

"Everyone who reads poetry knows it," Kate said between gurgles of laughter. "How wonderful that it is *you* who've written so famous a poem! Is Andrew Marvell your pen name?"

He glanced over at her, pouting. "How was I to know you knew it? And by heart!"

"Did you think I would not?" Her laughter dying, she shook her head at him. "Marvell is one of my most favorite poets. And if you'd read it all through you'd have understood his meaning is the opposite of your intention."

"I did read it through. I memorized the whole. I just didn't understand it."

"Didn't you? It's lovely, really." She sighed, and her eyes turned misty as she began to recite her favorite lines:

> " *'As lines, so loves oblique may well*
> *Themselves in every angle greet,*
> *But ours, so truly parallel,*
> *Though infinite, can never meet.'*

You see, my dear, he's saying that love is a longing that can't be fulfilled."

"Oh, is *that* what he means?" poor Percy asked in chagrin.

"Yes. And to try to pass his poetry off as your own is too ridiculous, Percy, even for you. That trick might work with one of your tavern wenches, but not with anyone who reads."

He scowled in self-disgust. "I should have guessed it wouldn't work. But Kate, don't you realize I'm at my wit's end? I don't know how to convince you to accept me."

Kate patted his knee. "Give it up, Percy. There is no manner of speech, no rhyme, no rhetoric of any sort that can possibly change my mind."

"I don't understand you, Kate." He turned to face her squarely. "You're well past the age of consent, are you not?"

"You know I am."

"And there's no other fellow who's captured your eye—or your heart, is there?"

"No, there is not."

"Then why not me? Am I so very dreadful in appearance?"

"Don't be a coxcomb. You know perfectly well you're top-of-the-trees."

That made him preen a bit. "Well, yes, I *have* been told I'm a right cool fish."

"No doubt by someone who admires gaudy waistcoats and shirtpoints up to the cheeks," Kate taunted, unable to help herself.

He stiffened. "You, Kate Rendell, have no appreciation of town fashion."

"If you're an example of it, no, I haven't," she retorted.

"I suppose," he muttered, "that you think me a complete fool."

"No, I don't think that at all. Except in your foolish persistence in offering for me."

"But I can't help it." He grasped her hands in a tight hold. "I love you to distraction. Have for years. And you're fond of me, I know you are. Damnation, woman, why won't you have me?"

"You have *me* at wit's end, Percy." She wrenched her hands free and glared at him. "This obstinate resistance to my refusal is more than my nature can bear. You've been a good companion from childhood, yes, but I've been telling you for years that you can never be more than that to me."

"How do you know you won't change?" he asked, looking at her pathetically.

"You must take my word that I know my own mind."

"I won't take your word. You cannot know the future. You may very well change your mind one of these days. I can coax you into it."

At that her patience snapped. She jumped to her feet. "Percival Greenway," she said icily, "if you cannot accept the fact that we'll never be lovers, I shall have to tell Havers to bar you from the house! And that's my last word on the subject."

Percy pulled himself up. "Very well," he pouted, "if

that's your last word, it will also be mine. Positively!"
With an exaggerated bow, like an actor in a drama, he
flounced to the door.

His melodramatic stride made such a comical contrast to the clownish exaggeration of his costume that
Kate felt a spasm of laughter rise in her throat. She
tried not to let it escape. "Good day, sir," she said with
a tiny gurgle, returning his bow.

He heard it and stood stock still. "You know, Kate,"
he said after a pause, his voice suddenly free of affec-
tation, "though you're very easy to *love,* you're quite
impossible to *like.* Positively!"

Kate stared after him, her mouth agape. Had he really said what she thought he'd said? She got to her
feet and took a step after him. "Percy! What—?"

But he'd stormed out of the room. The sound of his
footsteps was already fading as he clomped down the
hall. The sound of his angry voice, however, continued
to echo in the air. *Impossible to like* . . . that was what
he'd said. Those were his very words. Could they be
true? Was she really not likable?

She sank back down upon the sofa, her eyes fixed
on the empty doorway. For the second time that day,
she'd been given a cruel set down. And it wasn't even
noon!

THREE

꙳

Kate stalked into the sitting room where her mother sat close to the fire. "Mama," she said, dropping down on the hearth in front of her, "what's wrong with me?"

Lady Isabel, who'd been stitching away at her embroidery frame, stayed her hand. "Oh, dear, are you ill, my love?" she asked, her eyes showing more curiosity than alarm. Her ladyship was not one to fly into hysterics without sufficient reason. "Headachy? Feverish?"

"No, no, nothing like that. I'm quite well. Physically, anyway. What I mean is . . . is there something wrong with my character?"

"Your character?" Lady Isabel peered at her daughter in confusion.

"Yes, Mama, my character. My temperament. My nature."

"I don't know what you mean, Kate. You are a sensible, moral, entirely admirable woman. There's nothing *at all* wrong with your character." And with a dismissive wave of her hand, she resumed her sewing.

Kate studied her mother with some irritation. The woman had not turned fifty, yet she'd become completely absorbed by stitchery, an occupation befitting a much older woman. It was a passion that affected everything about her, even her appearance and the way she dressed. To Kate, it made her mama appear more grandmotherly than motherly. An enormous lace cap covered her hair, which—if she'd permitted anyone to see—had not a strand of gray. Her gown was a plain blue round-gown, which was bad enough, but what made it worse was the apron that covered it. It was a special apron Mama had designed herself. Its bodice was partitioned with a row of small pockets, each one bearing one skein of colored embroidery thread. A placket over her left breast was punctuated with needles of various sizes. Special magnifying glasses were perched on her nose. Was there any wonder that she appeared to be decades older than her years?

The needlework itself would be considered quite artistic, Kate supposed, by those who cared for such things, but to Kate it hardly seemed worth the enormous effort. The work required not only huge amounts of time but very complicated paraphernalia. There were not only skeins of thread to be untangled, needles constantly to be threaded, and the fabric stretched over an elongated rectangular frame, but Mama had concocted a four-legged, wheeled cart on which to carry her work. She made a ludicrous appearance pulling the clumsy thing behind her wherever she went!

What Kate didn't understand was what induced her mother to do all this. The entire household was already overstocked with her needlework. How much more did they need? Every upholstered chair had an embroidered doily on its back. Every room had at least three framed examples of her art. Every bed in all seven bedrooms sported a number of embroidered pillows. When would she decide that she'd created a sufficiency?

Kate sighed. "Must you keep sewing, Mama, when I'm trying to get a thoughtful answer from you?"

"I gave you a thoughtful answer. I said there's nothing wrong with your character."

"That was not a thoughtful answer. That was a mother's answer."

"But I *am* your mother. How else can I answer?"

"You can try to be a bit objective, can't you?"

"It's hard to be objective about one's own flesh and blood." Between stitches, Lady Isabel threw her daughter a quizzical look. "What made you ask such a strange question, my love?"

"The matter came up today," Kate replied glumly. "Twice!"

"A matter regarding your *character?*"

"Yes, and the assessments were not at all in agreement with yours.

The needle stopped again. "Are you saying that someone found fault with you?"

"Two someones. In one morning."

"Who on earth could possibly find fault with your

character?" her mother asked in perfect sincerity.

"Two gentlemen, Mama, neither of whom was obliged to look on me in a motherly way."

"And what fault did they find, I'd like to know!" the mother declared in offense.

Kate lifted her legs up on the hearth and wrapped her arms about them. "One said I was arrogant—"

"Did he, indeed! Who was the bounder?"

"Lord Ainsworth."

"Hmmmph!" Her ladyship's brows rose in offense. "What cheek! He's a fine one to talk about character! I understand from the on-dits in town that the fellow is a rake."

"A rake? Really?" Kate was surprised. "He didn't seem—"

"Why not?" Lady Isabel asked curiously. "Wasn't he handsome and dashing?"

Kate shut her eyes, trying to picture him again. "Somewhat handsome I suppose," she said, remembering her first reaction to him, "but not particularly dashing. He's losing his hair."

"Nevertheless, young ladies evidently fall at his feet. They say that Beatrice Hibbert threw over an earl in hope of Ainsworth, and all for naught. And I've heard that Miss Landers, Lady Elinor's second daughter, went into a decline when he didn't come up to scratch."

Kate shook her head. "But that's beside the point, Mama. Whatever his character, he certainly maligned mine. And, not three hours later, Percy did, too!"

"Percy? Percy Greenway, who's adored you since infancy? He called you arrogant?"

"Worse than that. He said that I was impossible to like!"

Her ladyship gaped. "He didn't!"

"He most certainly did. And with the utmost sincerity."

Lady Isabel stared at her daughter for a moment, and then, with brow wrinkled, resumed her sewing. "I suppose you said something cutting to the poor boy," she suggested.

"Nothing I haven't said a dozen times before."

"Hmm." Lady Isabel continued to stitch.

Kate cocked her head at her mother curiously. "What are you thinking, Mama? That there *is* something wrong with me?"

"From some points of view, I suppose that perhaps . . ." She paused and lowered her eyes.

"Well? Go on," Kate prodded.

Lady Isabel, her brow wrinkled, stuck her needle into the fabric and put the work aside. "Men do not take kindly to . . . to . . ." Here she hesitated again.

"Go on, Mama," Kate urged. "I need to hear some truths."

"To . . . strong women," the mother admitted reluctantly.

Kate's eyebrows lifted. "Strong?"

"You are strong, you know."

"I *don't* know. What does that mean?" She watched her mother's face intently. "Stubborn?"

"Well, yes, I suppose so."

"Arrogant, too?"

"I suppose some might find you so."

"Evidently some do," Kate muttered ruefully.

There was a moment of silence. Lady Isabel peered at her daughter, the affection in her eyes darkened with concern. "I don't believe being strong is so dreadful a fault," she said gently.

" 'Tis dreadful enough!"

The mother had no response. Kate stared into the fire thoughtfully while her mother picked up her embroidery frame and resumed her stitching. Kate, hearing the tiny pluck of the needle piercing the fabric, looked round in annoyance. "Really, Mama, I don't see why you must keep on sewing while I am trying to speak seriously to you."

"I'm sorry if it disturbs you, my love. But sewing is necessary to *my* character."

"Truly?" Kate asked curiously. "In what way?"

"Concentrating on my stitchery is my way of calming myself. If I didn't have my embroidery, I might not be able to maintain the serene manner I deem appropriate to a widow of my years and position."

"Serenity?" Kate's voice was scornful. "Is *that* what you find necessary to your character?"

"Yes, I do. Serenity, I believe, becomes me."

Her daughter opened her mouth to retort. *Serenity is a pale virtue*, she wanted to say. But on second thought she held her tongue. Perhaps it was not so pale. There was much to be said for being serene. A serene person was not arrogant, not disturbed, not disquieted, as she herself was at this moment. Her mother probably had the right of it.

Kate uncurled herself, got up, bent over her mother, and kissed her on her forehead. "Yes, Mama, serenity does become you," she said and headed for the door.

"Where are you off to?" Lady Isabel inquired serenely.

"To get a mirror. And then to the drawing room, to take a good look at the girl in the portrait. I want to compare us."

"To compare yourself to the girl in the Persian shawl?" Lady Isabel's eyebrows rose. "Whatever for?"

"To determine if my face has the same arrogance I see in hers."

FOUR

ᴧᴥᴥᴧ

Kate dreamed about him again. It was the third time that week. Three times she'd awakened with a slight feeling of depression, cobwebs of the same annoying dream clinging to the edges of her brain—hazy recollections of Harry Gerard, Lord Ainsworth, standing in the drawing room doorway mocking her. *How long,* she wondered as she crawled out of bed and scrambled for her robe, *will this irritating dream recur?*

The weeks that followed Lord Ainsworth's visit had been unpleasant ones for Kate. For one thing, the weather had turned cold, making the October air feel like January and spoiling her pleasure in her daily walks. For another, she often found herself in the drawing room, studying a painting that irked her to look at. She didn't understand why she was drawn to peer at it when, in all her years before, she'd not even bothered to notice it. Perhaps her sudden fascination with it had come from the disquieting awareness that the arrogance in the painted face somehow reflected something unpleasant in her own. *Is that arrogance,* she found herself wondering, *the reason Percy finds me impossible to like?*

But the most unpleasant part of the past several weeks was the recurrence of the memory of her interview with Lord Ainsworth. The stupid *contretemps* seemed to have lodged itself firmly and permanently into her inner being. If she'd been in a proper frame of mind, she'd have forgotten the incident long since. Lately, however, something seemed to be wrong with her. She had only to shut her eyes and there he'd be, Harry Gerard, Lord Ainsworth, standing before her, his mouth curled in a slight, sardonic smile, and his light eyes laughing at her. What was he doing, lingering about in her memory that way?

She thrust her feet into a pair of fleecy slippers, padded over to the window, and drew aside the draperies. A quick glance at the still, snowy landscape gave her no cheer. Even the air seemed winter-gray despite the wan efforts of the sun to make itself seen through thin clouds. She shivered and drew her robe closer about her. It would be another bone-chilling day.

The sound made by the drawing aside of the draperies must have alerted her abigail, for the door opened and Megan stuck her head in. "Ah, y're awake," the maid said cheerfully. "Good mornin' t' ye."

"Mmmmph," Kate responded glumly. Megan's perky Irish-red curls and lively spirits affected Kate in the same way that a sudden bright light affects eyes long accustomed to the dark—she winced at the sight of the girl. "Go away!"

In response, Megan merely smiled more broadly and stepped into the room. "Sounds like ye need a bit o' cheerin'. I'll bring the purple muslin wi' the big sleeves fer ye to wear. That'll brighten yer mood."

"No it won't. Do go away, Megan. I don't want to dress just yet. Has Mama gone down?"

" 'Bout 'alf an hour ago." She eyed her mistress's robe in disapproval. "Ye don' want t' go down like that, do ye, Miss Kate? Ye won't be warm enough."

"Good God, girl, stop being motherly. I'll be fine. And when I decide to dress, I'll do it myself, so you needn't bother hanging about waiting for me."

"Oh, aye," the maid sneered. "As if ye cin do up those buttons by yersel'. I'll be back." And before Kate could could retort, she scooted out of the room.

Kate glared at the door for a moment. Then, after making quick work of her ablutions, she wrapped herself in a warmer robe and took herself down to breakfast.

Her mother, fully dressed and aproned for her needlework, sat at the table reading the day's mail. She, too, did not looked pleased. "I've a letter from your uncle Charles," she said, frowning.

Kate was surprised. A letter from Uncle Charles usually filled her mother with delight. Lady Isabel had the greatest affection for her brother-in-law, Charles Quigley, now Lord Rendell. They had always been good friends, and Uncle Charles could always be counted on for aid when trouble came upon them.

When Viscount Rendell died, Claydon Castle in Nor-folk, Rendall Hall in Suffolk, and all the other Rendell properties went to Charles, but he insisted that his brother's widow and her daughter continue in posses-sion of Rendell Hall. He'd made it quite clear that he and Aunt Madge were content enough with Claydon and that Rendell Hall and acreage were to be used entirely for his sister's benefit. There were not many brothers-in-law half so generous.

"What's wrong?" Kate asked as she took her place and reached for the teapot.

"He writes that we must come to him next week. We're to plan to spend an entire fortnight at Claydon. It seems that your aunt Madge is preparing for all manner of festivities. What a bore."

"Why do you say it will be a bore? If Aunt Madge is planning festivities, you may be sure a ball is in order. That means a coterie from London is sure to be there. Some of your own cronies, certainly. You will have a delicious time gossiping and learning the latest on-dits from town."

"I don't gossip. And I've long since lost interest in the news from town. I'm of an age when I enjoy noth-ing so much as quiet days like this, safe and at peace in my own home."

"Of an age? What nonsense!" Kate eyed her mother in annoyance. At this moment a stream of pale winter sun, slanting in from the tall, east-facing windows, was haloing her mother's dark hair. She looked positively lovely, her daughter thought. Vigorous and youthful, with smooth skin and full cheeks, she seemed at least a decade younger than her not-quite-fifty years. Why, Kate asked herself, was her mother so reluctant to do something with her life? It was time Kate herself took some action. Her mother was too young to wither away into loneliness. What the woman needed was a companion, preferably a man.

The more she thought about it, the more sure Kate became that it was time for action. There were many widows not half so attractive as her mother who'd found a second love in their lives. And surely there were many elderly gentlemen who would suit. Kate would find a second husband for her mother or die trying. And the house-party at Claydon was the perfect place to start. "Really, Mama, I won't endure having you speak that way," she said. "You're much too young to consider retiring into an armchair for the rest of your life. I don't see why you insist on behaving like an elderly dotard."

"I insist on behaving as I see fit," Lady Isabel retorted.

Kate shrugged. "Nevertheless, we will do as Uncle Charles asks and accept his invitation."

Lady Isabel frowned at her. "Will we, indeed?"

"Yes, we will. Let me have the letter. I shall write our acceptance this very morning."

"There you go again, deciding everything yourself," her mother remarked. Nevertheless, with a sigh of surrender, she passed the letter over to her daughter as ordered.

Kate's face fell. "*Do* I decide everything myself?" she asked, half to herself. Could planning for her mother's future be called decision-making? And was making decisions a sign that she was indeed as arrogant as Harry Gerard had suggested? It was a sobering thought.

"Yes, you do," her mother said. "You choose the menus, scold the delinquent housemaids, choose the fabric for new curtains, figure out what we can afford to offer as Boxing Day gifts to the servants, select whom to invite for tea when—" But at that moment she caught a glimpse of the alarm in her daughter's eyes. "However, I must admit," she added, seeking to soften her remarks, "I encourage you to do so. Because you're usually right."

Kate bit her lip. Had she the right to interfere in her mother's life? "I really don't wish to make decisions for you, Mama. If you truly don't want to go to Uncle Charles', I'll make our excuses."

"No, no," Lady Isabel admitted, "I was only blathering. Of course we must go. I wouldn't offend Charles for the world."

Kate nodded and let her eyes wander over the letter in her hand. "It sounds as if they're planning an out-and-out gala," she remarked as she nibbled at her toast. "I wonder why."

"I wondered that myself."

Kate paused in the act of pouring her tea. "It isn't someone's birthday, is it?"

"No. The tone suggests a much more exciting event than a mere birthday." Lady Isabel put down her cup and rose from her chair. "Well, there's no use surmising. We'll learn what it is soon enough. Meanwhile, I shall retire to my easy chair while I still may."

Kate was studying the letter with brows knit, but suddenly the puzzled expression cleared. "I'll wager I know what it is!" she declared.

Her mother, starting from the table, looked back at Kate over her shoulder. "You do?"

"It's Deirdre. She gone and got herself betrothed."

Lady Isabel's mouth dropped open. "Good heavens, do you think so?"

"Yes, I do. What better reason for Uncle Charles to hold a gala?" Kate smiled for the first time that morning. Her cousin Deirdre was a favorite with her, quite like a younger sister. "Wouldn't it be delightful if Deirdre were betrothed?"

"Humph," grunted her mother, "why delightful? She's nineteen, five years younger than you. I shall have to spend the entire fortnight thinking of excuses to make to my friends about why *she's* betrothed and *you* are not." And with that, she strolled from the room, her embroidery cart trundling along behind her, oblivious of the resentful glare Kate threw at her back.

FIVE

❧

The two ladies, accompanied by Megan, the coachman, his tiger, and a footman, set out in two coaches for Claydon Castle at noon. The first coach carried the three females. The second—a shabby old laudalet driven by the footman—was loaded with almost a dozen trunks, portmanteaux and bandboxes, and the wooden, four-legged, wheeled contraption that her ladyship used to hold her embroidery frame. Because the journey—a mere forty-eight miles—usually required no more than five hours, they expected to arrive at Claydon before tea. Their plans were overturned, however, by a pair of unfortunate circumstances. First, a sudden, quite heavy snowfall slowed them down between Mendlesham and Scole. And then, no sooner had the sky cleared and they'd started out again, when the ladies' carriage lurched to the side with a frightening crash. A wheel had broken. The coachman signaled the driver of the other carriage to go on ahead while he made a temporary repair and coaxed the crippled vehicle ever so slowly to the nearest town. There the ladies were made as comfortable as possible at a shabby inn while a wheelwright was summoned to put on a new wheel.

"We should have stayed at home, as I wished," Lady Isabel remarked as they warmed themselves at a smoky fire. "We could have come down with Percy on Saturday. He prides himself on the excellence of his carriages. He'd have taken us in his barouche. He would not have broken a wheel."

"What do you mean?" Kate asked in surprise. "Has Percy been invited?"

"Yes, for the weekend."

"But they hardly know him. Whatever possessed Uncle Charles to invite him?"

"Perhaps it was Madge who did it. There will be a ball, I suspect, and single gentlemen are an asset at a ball. Besides, she probably felt she was doing it as a favor to you."

"As a favor to me? Good heavens, why?"

"Your aunt is convinced that Percy is your last, best chance."

Kate stiffened in offense. "Are you suggesting that she enticed him all the way to Claydon so that he'd be near me? He lives *next door* to us! Does my aunt imagine I'll find him more attractive at the castle than I do at home?" Disgusted, Kate rolled her eyes heavenward. "May God forgive her, for I won't."

It was hours after dark when they finally arrived at

their destination. As the coach drew up to the entrance, the heavy doors swung wide, and Charles and his wife ran down the stone steps to greet them. "We've been worried sick," Madge cried, embracing her sister-in-law warmly. "Your man arrived with your baggage hours ago. He was certain you were right behind him!"

"Hush, Madge," Uncle Charles said, putting an arm about his niece's shoulders and kissing her cheek fondly, "let's get them inside, out of this chill."

As an army of servants descended to deal with the baggage, the host and hostess led the ladies up the huge stone stairway and into the hall. Madge Quigley, large in both height and girth, was panting from the effort of climbing the stairs, but that did not still her tongue. "You'll be glad to . . . know, Isabel," she informed her sister-in-law between deep breaths, "that some of your . . . friends are . . . coming for the weekend. Miss Gladmore, your old . . . friend from school . . . and Lady Stockmore. And the Gerards . . . and the Tyndales are already here." She paused, pressed her hands against her heaving chest, and, having caught her breath, went on. "They've been waiting to greet you all afternoon, but they're all dressing for dinner now."

"Then we'll go up at once and change," Lady Isabel said.

"Good idea," Charles agreed. "We don't want to keep everyone waiting to dine."

The two visitors started up the stairs. When they were out of earshot of their hosts, Lady Isabel asked her daughter, sotto voce, "Who on earth are the Gerards and the Tyndales?"

Kate, who'd felt a strange clench of the muscles of her stomach at hearing the name Gerard, managed to shrug. "I haven't the faintest idea," she said, throwing her mother a glance of bland innocence, "but isn't Lord Ainsworth a Gerard? He wouldn't be . . . couldn't be . . . related to these guests, could he?"

"Ainsworth? The rake?" Lady Isabel wrinkled her brow, trying to remember. "Oh, yes, I think he is a Gerard. But I doubt if he'd be here. Not the sort of party for a rake."

Kate, climbing up ahead, was about to answer when a movement on the landing just above her caught her eye. A man sauntered by. One quick glance was all she got of him, but it was enough to make her gasp. Could it really have been Lord Ainsworth himself?

Almost at once he was gone. There was a sound of a door closing. She could not be sure whom she'd seen. But the mere suggestion that it might be he, froze her to the spot.

Her mother came up behind her. "Is something wrong, Kate? You look pale."

She shook her head. "No, nothing," and she proceeded up the stairs. "But perhaps this *is* the sort of party to attract a rake."

Alone in her room, she stood stock still in the center of the floor, as if in a trance. Her cloak slid unheeded from her shoulders. *It couldn't be!* she told herself. What could Ainsworth possibly be doing in this house? It was a trick of her mind. Hearing the name

Gerard had made her imagine him. But it was foolishness. Gerard was not a particularly uncommon name. She should give herself a proper scolding for allowing herself to see him at every turn.

But what if it really *were* he? What would it mean? Would she have to smile at him in the sitting room, sit across from him at the table making polite conversation, play silver loo with him in the evenings? It was all too dreadful to contemplate.

What on earth, she wondered, *was his connection to the family in this house?* Was there a painting that Uncle Charles owned that he'd come to see? She knew the artwork in this house, and she could not think of one that resembled *Girl with Persian Shawl.* It wasn't likely that he was a friend of Aunt Madge. The only answer seemed to be . . . *Deirdre!*

She shut her eyes in agony as the horrible idea burst upon her. *Harry Gerard, Lord Ainsworth, was Deirdre's betrothed!*

SIX

❧✦❧

Megan, a green brocaded-silk evening dress over her arm, stood with elbows akimbo, watching her mistress stare at herself in the dressing-table mirror. "There's somethin' amiss," she declared firmly. "I cin see it in yer face."

Kate tossed her a frown. "I tell you, nothing at all's amiss."

"You needn't pitch me your gammon," the maid sneered. "I know ye too well. I cin tell when somethin's eatin' at ye."

"It's nothing," Kate insisted, getting up from the dressing table. "I just don't know what to do with this hair. We've no time to put it up, and it's too unruly to leave it hanging down like this."

"Sit back down. I'll tie it back with a pretty ribbon. It'll be fine," the maid assured her.

Kate sighed again and let Megan deal with her hair.

The few moments it took to brush and tie back the unruly brown locks—an irritating thatch that was neither smoothly straight nor charmingly curly—helped Kate to get hold of herself. *Somehow,* she swore to herself, *I will manage to behave with composure. When the shocking news that Deirdre has betrothed herself to that bounder Lord Ainsworth is announced tonight, I will applaud with the same enthusiasm as all the others.* There was no reason for her to feel such agitation. Neither Lord Ainsworth nor the betrothal itself had anything to do with her.

She stood up and let Megan help her into the gown. This green brocade was a favorite of hers. The ruffled lace at the neck and the slim, long sleeves made her feel stately. Being dressed with such restrained dignity would help her get through the ordeal of this evening.

Megan had just started on the back buttons when a knock sounded at the door. "Kate?" came a voice from the corridor. "It's Deirdre. May I come in?"

Kate ran to the door and threw it open. "Deirdre!" she exclaimed, opening her arms.

The girl in the doorway threw herself into them. "Oh, Kate! I'm so glad you've come! I couldn't *wait* to tell you—"

"Stop, my dear," Kate laughed, holding her at arm's length. "First let me look at you! I haven't seen you these six months."

"Never mind that!" the girl cried, grasping both Kate's hands, "I must tell you my news!"

But Kate was already studying her. Deirdre looked lovely, the sparkle in her blue eyes adding zest to the sweetness of her face. Her nineteen years had brought her to full bloom, her figure slim and yet softly rounded. She'd braided her fair hair in a coronet that emphasized her full cheeks and dimpled chin. Already dressed for dinner in a bare-shouldered, light-blue crepe gown that shimmered with silver threads, she veritably exuded joyousness. "Heavens," Kate exclaimed admiringly, "you are breathtaking!"

"Per'aps you should've worn yer lavender Florentine with the bare shoulders," Megan muttered to her mistress, eyeing Deirdre's gown enviously. "Seems dinner'll be more poshy than I thought."

Kate glared at her. "You may *go*, Megan," she said pointedly.

"But I ain't finished buttonin' ye," the maid objected.

"I can do it," Deirdre offered at once.

Megan, defeated, shrugged and took herself off.

Deirdre, who hadn't dropped hold of Kate's hands, drew her to the bedstead and pulled her cousin down beside her. "You won't believe what's happened, Kate," she exclaimed breathlessly. "I'm in love!"

Kate felt her fingers clench. "Are you, sweetheart?"

"Head over heels! Oh, Kate, wait till you meet him! He's *glorious*. As handsome as a dream prince, with a lovely smile and the broadest shoulders. And he's so clever and sweet natured, and he has the most divine eyes!"

"My!" Kate said, forcing a grin. "He sounds too good to be believed."

"You'll believe it when you meet him."

"I'm sure I will. Though I hope you don't expect me to fall at his feet. It's enough that you are top-over-tail. It wouldn't do for both of us to feel that way."

"You're teasing me, I know. But he really is just too magnificent for words! And, Kate, the very best part is, he feels the same toward me. He's *offered* for me!"

"Has he?"

"Yes! And Papa has accepted him. They're to announce the betrothal *tonight!*"

"Tonight?" Kate lifted the girl's chin and smiled at her fondly. "No wonder you're glowing like a mid-summer moon."

"Am I? Well, I suppose I am. Tonight is special, after all, even if it will only be a small family dinner."

"Small? Your mother said there would be two other families. Tyndales and Gerards, she said."

"Yes, but only two Tyndales and three Gerards," she explained. "With the five of us, that makes only ten for dinner."

"Ten is quite enough to make the occasion special," Kate assured her.

"Yes, of course. Quite enough." Deirdre threw her arms about Kate's neck and held her tightly. "Oh, Kate, I'm so happy! And you, you know, are my best friend in all the world. Your being here with me tonight makes everything perfect!"

Kate, trying to overcome her conflicting emotions, returned her cousin's embrace. "Dearest Deirdre," she whispered into the girl's ear, "it all sounds wonderful. I wish you the greatest happiness."

SEVEN

~~~~

After Deirdre floated out of the room on her blue-and-silver cloud, Megan came back in, the lavender Florentine silk gown with the low décolletage over her arm. Kate frowned at her. "Really, Megan, you are a nuisance. I don't want to change my gown."

"Yes, ye do," the maid insisted. "Ye don' want t' go down lookin' like Miss Deirdre's maiden aunt, do ye?"

Kate was appalled "Is that what I look like? Her maiden aunt?" She stared at herself in the dressing-table mirror for a moment. Then, with a shrug of defeat, she began to unbutton the green long-sleeved gown.

Because she'd taken the time to change to the lavender gown, Kate was the last to join the group assembled in the drawing room before dinner. Pausing in the doorway, she glanced round the room. There

were not many familiar faces. Of course she knew the
elderly butler, Pruitt. He'd been in the family since
long before Kate was born. He was now serving
glasses of sherry to a trio of ladies sitting near the
fire—her aunt Madge, a tiny but distinguished-looking
elderly lady in a purple velvet half-cape, and her
mother. Kate noticed that her mother had dressed for
this occasion in a puce-colored lace gown and, instead
of her widow's cap, had placed a jeweled comb in her
hair. Aunt Madge must have warned her that the evening would be special. It pleased Kate to see her
mother looking so stylish and enjoying lively conversation without her ever-present needlework in her
hands.

On the far side of the room she spied Deirdre, seated
in an armchair. Perched on the arm was Lord Ainsworth. But Deirdre was not conversing with him. Her
head was turned toward another young man, a bushy-
haired fellow who was leaning over the back of her
chair. Ainsworth seemed to take notice of Kate's arrival, but she, though she would have liked to know
if he recognized her, found herself unable to meet his
eyes. She knew full well, as she dropped her eyes from
his, that her act was cowardly. This behavior—quite
like a simpering miss—was not her usual style. *What's
wrong with me?* she asked herself.

She had no time to analyze this distressing reaction,
for her uncle spied her at that moment. "Ah, Kate,"
he cried jovially, "there you are at last!" He rose from
the sofa where he'd been sitting with an impressive-

looking gentleman and came across the room to her. "Let me make you known to everyone."

Uncle Charles put an arm about her waist and led her to the group at the fireplace. Addressing the unknown lady in the purple cape, he said, "Your ladyship, may I present my niece, Miss Kate Rendell? Kate, this is Charlotte, Lady Ainsworth."

Kate, wondering if this might be Lord Ainsworth's mother, made a bow. Her ladyship was a tiny, wizened woman who nevertheless sat up straight as a queen, the majestic effect enhanced by her bright eyes, her abundant white hair tucked under a widow's cap, and the velvet cape that covered her narrow shoulders like a royal mantle. In the manner of a benign monarch, she smiled up at Kate and held out her hand. "I'm delighted to meet you, my dear," she said warmly. "I've heard much in praise of you."

Kate felt herself blush as she took the wrinkled hand. "You shouldn't take my mother's word for my character, your ladyship. She's bound to be partial."

"It was not from your mother that I heard it," her ladyship said with a twinkle.

"Oh?" Kate responded with real interest. "Who could have—?"

"Come Kate," her uncle cut in rudely, "you must meet the others."

Kate could do nothing but bow again and follow where he led.

She was next presented to the elderly gentleman who'd been conversing with her uncle, Sir Edward Tyndale. His dignified manner, overly formal attire, and powdered hair showed him to be determinedly old-fashioned. Sir Edward rose and kissed her hand gallantly, just as he'd probably done for half a century. Yet there was something in his expression—a lively brightness in the eyes—that made Kate like him at once.

His son, the Honorable Leonard Tyndale, was the fellow who'd been standing behind Deirdre's chair. His mop of auburn hair topped a cheerful face, full cheeks sprinkled with freckles, an upturned nose, and a mouth showing a decided propensity to smile. His manner, too, was unaffected and good-humored. The enthusiastic way he came forward to shake her hand put Kate immediately at ease with him. The two Tyndales, she decided, would be pleasant company.

Then Uncle Charles turned to Ainsworth. "Harry," he said jovially, "come and meet my niece."

Ainsworth rose from his perch. "But we've already met," he told Charles with a grin. "How do you do, Miss Rendell?"

"Very well, thank you, my lord," Kate replied, uncomfortably aware of a strange wobbling of her knees. His lordship was even more disturbingly attractive than he'd seemed in her reveries, and, despite his receding hairline, every bit as handsome as Deirdre had claimed. And when he flashed his particularly infectious grin, it was as if an inner light suddenly came on and lit up his whole face. But at this moment there was a slightly mocking look in his eyes—a look she remembered well—and as irritating right now as it had been when he'd given her that set down in her drawing room.

"How on earth do you two know each other?" Uncle Charles wanted to know.

"I visited Rendell Hall a few weeks ago," Ainsworth explained. "I went to see a painting—*Girl with Persian Shawl.*"

"Ah, yes," Charles said, nodding. "A lovely work, that."

"Miss Rendell thought I wanted to steal it from her."

Kate glared at him. "I did *not* think—"

But Charles cut her off, for the butler appeared at his elbow at that moment. "Do have some sherry, Kate," he said, taking a glass from the tray.

She took the glass, grateful for the interruption. "But someone is missing," she remarked after taking a sip. "Deirdre told me there would be three Gerards at the table. I've met only two."

"My brother, Benjamin," Harry Gerard said. "He's in the library, sulking."

"Sulking?"

"Benjy's only fourteen. He's disappointed that there's no one his age present to keep him company."

"Poor fellow. That *is* too bad," Kate said.

"I'll send Pruitt to roust him out," Charles said. "We'll be going in to dinner in a few moments."

"Let me go, Uncle Charles," Kate offered. "I'll introduce myself and bring him back with me." And before anyone could object, she swung on her heel and swept out of the room, depositing her sherry glass on a table near the door as she passed.

The castle corridors had high ceilings, wood-paneled walls, and floors of polished stone. Despite the ensconced torches that provided light at measured intervals, the hall was dark and cold. As Kate hurried along toward the library, which was a good distance away, she shivered from the chill, regretting for a moment having offered to fetch the boy. She regretted even more having changed into this bare-shouldered gown.

She hadn't gone far when she heard footsteps behind her, and then a voice. "Miss Rendell, wait."

She turned to discover Lord Ainsworth striding after her. "Your lordship?"

He came up beside her. "These halls are deucedly drafty. I've brought you a cape."

"My! How very thoughtful of you!" she said with sincere gratitude as he draped it over her shoulders.

"I cannot take credit. Actually, it was my grandmother's suggestion. When she saw me set out to follow you, she thrust it at me."

"Oh!" She looked down at the garment and recognized the purple cape Lady Ainsworth had been wearing. So that lovely woman was his *grandmother*. But why had he permitted her to give up her cape? "Good heavens, she was *wearing* it!" Kate cried in chagrin. "How could you permit her to—?"

"She said you will need it more than she. She assured me she was quite warm enough at the fire."

"I see. In that case, I'm immensely grateful to her.

This corridor belongs in an ice palace." She drew the cape tightly around her shoulders, enjoying the warmth. As she drew in a contented breath, his other words came to her mind. "But what was it you said before? That you set out to *follow* me? Why?"

"For no ulterior motive, I assure you. In the game of love, if that is what you thought I was playing, I am not a participant. The reason I followed you was merely that I thought it proper for me to escort you and introduce you to Benjy myself."

"Did you, indeed?" She peered up at him suspiciously. She'd hadn't forgotten his disparaging remark about her to her uncle, and she certainly hadn't forgotten the insult he'd given her at Rendell Hall. He obviously didn't like her. So what sort of game was he playing? Did rakes believe they should capture every female in their vicinity? "Escorting me is quite unnecessary, my lord," she said.

"From a lady's point of view, perhaps. But I like to adhere to a gentleman's standards."

"Not always, I think," she retorted pointedly.

He looked at her blankly, but only for a moment. "Ah," he said, remembering, "you're thinking of our conversation when I called at Rendell Hall. If I was ungentlemanly to you that day, Miss Rendell, I most sincerely apologize." His lips curved in a small smile. "Although I think you should admit that you were at least partially to blame."

She lowered her eyes. "I admit nothing." She would not give him the satisfaction of agreeing, even if he had the right of it. Anyway, she told herself, this sort of conversation would not do. It would be best for her peace of mind to rid herself of his company. "But, my lord," she suggested pleasantly, "wouldn't it be more gentlemanly if you returned to the drawing room?"

"More gentlemanly? Why?"

"To be available to escort your betrothed in to dinner?"

"What?" His lordship blinked at her bewilderedly.

"Your betrothed. Deirdre."

"What on earth are you talking about, Miss Rendell?"

She smiled at him knowingly. "Come now, my lord, you needn't play the innocent. I know all about it."

He peered down at her in amazement. "I don't understand. What is it that you know all about?"

"About you and Deirdre. Deirdre told me herself."

"Told you?" His brows drew together in perplexity. "Told you about—?"

"About your engagement, yes. You needn't pretend with me, you know. Deirdre confided the whole to me."

"The whole *what?*"

"The whole. That you and she are betrothed, of course."

"Deirdre told you that she and *I*—?"

"There's no need to deny it," Kate cut in, patting his arm reassuringly. "I understand that it's supposed to be kept secret until the announcement tonight, but she and I are closer than mere cousins. We're very good friends, and she couldn't keep me in the dark."

"Let me understand this," Lord Ainsworth said,

cocking his head at her. "Deirdre told you that she and I are betrothed. She mentioned me by name, did she?"

"She didn't have to."

"I see." He gave a little snort.

"Are you annoyed with her? You mustn't be. She knew I wouldn't say anything."

"I am not annoyed, ma'am. But I'd—"

"Then you mustn't keep her waiting for you. I'm quite capable of fetching your brother by myself. Do go back to the drawing room."

He shook his head in amazement. "I must say, Miss Rendell, that your character is remarkably . . . er . . ."

She saw that same, ironically amused look in his eyes. "Remarkably what?" she asked defensively.

"Remarkably consistent."

She stiffened. "I don't know what you mean by that," she said coldly, "but I know you don't mean it as a compliment."

"Why do you assume that?'

"From that mocking look in your eye. Am I right?"

He flashed one of his disarming grins. "It would not be gentlemanly to say." And with a quick bow and a wave of his hand, he turned and strolled back down the hall.

EIGHT

❧

The boy in the library was staring morosely out a tall window, as if he could really see something out there in the darkening landscape. Kate, observing him from the doorway, let out a surprised "Oh!" She'd expected him to be tall for his age and dark-haired like his brother, as indeed he was. But what she hadn't expected was that his right arm would be in a sling.

At the sound of her cry, he wheeled about, his eyes (light, like his brother's) showing the fear of a hunted animal.

She stepped over the threshold. "I startled you," she said. "I'm sorry. You see, they didn't tell me about your arm."

"Beg pardon, ma'am?"

She smiled and offered her hand. "I'm not ma'am. I'm Kate, our host's niece. If you're Benjy, I've been sent to fetch you."

"I'm Benjy," he said wanly, taking her hand in his left. "How do you do?"

"Evidently I do better than you. What happened to your arm?"

"It's my shoulder. I wrenched it playing cricket. At school, you know." He dropped both her hand and his eyes. "They won't let me back for another six weeks. They say it'll be mended by then."

"That *is* too bad." She cocked an eyebrow at him. "You must like school a great deal, to be so downhearted at missing it."

"I didn't used to think so, but it's a great deal better than hanging about with . . . with . . ."

"With older people?"

"I meant no offense," he muttered, shoving back a lock of hair from his forehead. "It's just that there's no one near my age either at home or here for me to talk to, and there's nothing to do. Even Harry won't let me ride or go shooting with him as he used to."

"I suppose he wants to keep you from further injury," she suggested.

"I suppose," the boy sighed, "but it's a blasted nuisance to be kept wrapped in cotton wool."

"I know just how you feel," Kate said, taking his good arm and leading him to the door. "I'm in the same situation myself."

"You?"

"Oh, not wrapped in cotton wool. I didn't mean that. I meant about having no one about to talk to or do things with. My cousin Deirdre is my friend, but I fear she'll be too busy to keep me company this time. And there's no one else . . ." She smiled down at the boy sympathetically. "I, too, will have little to do."

They walked down the hall in sympathetic silence. "Of course," Kate added, "we can keep each other company, if you'd permit it. I don't suppose you'd enjoy a game of spillikins or bilbocatch, what with your arm tied up—and they're too childish anyway. But I can teach you copper loo—"

"I'm wizard at copper loo," Benjy said eagerly, "but we'd need a few more to play."

"Ecarte, then. Do you know the game? It only requires two."

Benjy's face brightened. "Would you really play with me?"

"Of course. For real pennies, if you wish."

By the time they reached the drawing room, they'd arranged a time and a place for the game. Benjy was actually smiling. His brother noticed it at once and started toward them, but at that moment Aunt Madge called out his name. "Lord Ainsworth, your arm," she clarioned. The procession into the dining room was beginning to form.

Uncle Charles approached Kate and offered his arm, but she shook her head. "I already have an escort, Uncle Charles. You did say you'd take me in, didn't you, Benjy?"

Benjy beamed. "Yes, ma'am, I mean Kate." And, preening proudly, he led her into the dining room.

It seemed to Kate that everyone at the dinner table was bubbling with excitement. Conversation flourished all around her. Deirdre, seated to the right of her father, bestowed a radiant smile on everyone, except when Ainsworth, who was seated next to her, leaned over to her to whisper in her ear and make her laugh. The old-fashioned Sir Edward seemed to be doing the same for Kate's mother, who was apparently enjoying herself immensely. Kate, though seated between Leonard and Benjy, and getting plenty of attention from both, had a hard time responding to all the good humor. Her insides seemed to be tied up in knots.

She knew the cause: She did *not* want to hear the announcement that would soon be made. In spite of having told herself over and over that the matter did not concern her, in spite of having promised herself that she would cheer as enthusiastically as everyone else when the words were said . . . in spite of all that, her spirits were depressed. But to be depressed at the happiness of someone she cared for dismayed her. She disliked herself for these ungracious feelings. *What is happening to me?* she asked herself. Ever since her first encounter with Lord Ainsworth, she'd become a disappointment to herself. She was not the warmhearted, independent, strong-minded creature she'd thought she was.

When the second course was removed, the footmen came forward and set delicate glass goblets at every place. As Pruitt circled the table, filling them with sparkling wine, Uncle Charles tapped on his glass and stood up. Kate braced herself for what was to come.

Uncle Charles cleared his throat awkwardly. "As you may already have suspected," he said, tugging at his neckcloth with embarrassment, "there's a special reason my lady and I have brought you all together tonight. It's an announcement that I'm sure will surprise and delight everyone. But since I do not pride myself on my oratory, I'm going to call on someone with more talent for this sort of thing than I have to make the announcement for me. Harry, please."

Ainsworth stood up as Charles sat down. "Thank you, Charles, I am honored." He turned and smiled at everyone looking up at him. "Ladies and gentlemen, a mere month ago I would not have been a likely choice to make this announcement, for its subject is love, and in the game of love I was a staunch cynic. Love, to me, was a delusion—a mistaken conviction that one particular man or woman differs from all others. At its best, I thought, love was a will-o'-the-wisp that forever eluded one's grasp, a mirage that everyone swears is real but very few have actually seen." Here he turned his gaze on Deirdre. "But now I've seen it with my own eyes, and I know how wrong I've been."

Kate felt a twinge in her throat. *What a lovely way to declare himself*, she thought. *How Deirdre must be enjoying this!*

"You, too, can see love shining forth tonight," Ainsworth continued, "for the signs are unmistakable. Like a cough or an itch, love cannot be hidden. It gleams from the eyes of the lovely Deirdre like encapsulated star-shine. And where will we find the answering gleam? You needn't look very far, for it, too, is unmistakable. In the eyes, of course, of my cousin, Leonard Tyndale, who, though a good-enough fellow, doesn't nearly deserve such a beautiful bride."

Here Lord Ainsworth flicked a gloating glance at Kate, but she was so overset by what she'd just heard that she barely noticed. All she knew was that she'd heard something surprising ... something that was causing the knot in her stomach to dissolve and her fingers to tremble so badly she had to clench them in her lap. It seemed that her body understood something that her brain did not yet grasp. What had just been said? That Deirdre was to be *Leonard's* bride? Had she heard aright?

Ainsworth, meanwhile, was lifting his glass. "Yes, it may well be that our Leonard doesn't deserve the lovely Deirdre. But love has its own eyes. Because Deirdre chose to accept him, we can do nothing but wish him well. Let us raise our glasses and drink to this happiest of betrothals. To Deirdre and Leonard. May they have years of joy."

And amid loud laughter and applause, the listeners got to their feet, raised their glasses, and drank to the seated pair.

Kate got to her feet, too, but she didn't know how she'd managed it. Her brain was in a whirl. *Leonard?* Was *he* the magnificent, handsome, broad-shouldered specimen Deirdre had so glowingly described in Kate's bedroom? Was Deirdre truly betrothed to Leonard Tyndale? Kate could hardly believe her ears!

But she'd heard it clearly enough. There was no mistaking it now. Young Tyndale was the groom-to-be.

And Harry Gerard, Lord Ainsworth, was not.

NINE

❦

While the men enjoyed their after-dinner brandies, the women adjourned to the drawing room and circled the glowing Deirdre like doting grandmamas about a newborn babe, giggling and embracing her and offering their excited congratulations. They plied her with all sorts of questions about the forthcoming wedding, but Deirdre, though blushing prettily, shook her head and let her mother answer for her. "I'm not thinking beyond the ball on Saturday," Madge told them. "After that, there will be plenty of time to make wedding plans."

The gentlemen soon rejoined the ladies, and Charles immediately began to arrange for a game of whist. Lady Ainsworth excused herself. "I think I shall retire for the night," she said, rising. "Benjy, give me your good arm and escort me upstairs. You, too, ought to go to bed. You need adequate rest to insure a good recovery."

The boy threw Kate an expression of helpless disgust at his grandmother's words, but he did as he was told. After the pair had bid the assemblage good night and left the room, a card table was set up, and Charles, Madge, Isabel, and Sir Edward took places for the game. Deirdre and her newly affianced lover, arms entwined, sat down beside each other on the sofa near the fire and gazed lovingly into each other's eyes. This left Kate with no company but Lord Ainsworth himself.

She found the situation unfortunate. How could she face his lordship with equilibrium after having made the humiliating mistake of assuming he was the prospective bridegroom? The only means of escape was for her, too, to retire for the night. She went up to her mother's chair. "I think I'll go up to bed also," she whispered in her ear.

"Very well, dear," her mother murmured, patting her arm but not looking up from her cards.

"Good night, all," Kate said to the other players and started for the door.

Lord Ainsworth followed her. "Surely it's too early for bed," he said, taking her arm and smiling down at her.

"It's been a long day," Kate said, trying unsuccessfully to slip her arm from his grasp.

"Then you must let me escort you to your room." Ignoring her resistant tug, he pulled her arm through his and walked with her out the door.

Once outside the drawing room, she flicked a glance up at his face. *Why was he doing this?* she asked herself. Did he want to gloat at her humiliation? He was looking down at her with that ironic gleam in his eyes—the very expression that irritated her from the first day of their acquaintance. "I suppose you're feeling quite proud of yourself," she said, wrenching her arm free.

His eyebrows rose innocently. "Proud, ma'am?"

"For having made a fool of me again." Tossing her head, she walked away from him toward the stairway.

With his long stride, he had no difficulty keeping up with her. "Not proud, my dear," he said. "Only amused."

"That's the purpose of fools, isn't it? To amuse people?" The question was belligerent, but soon her eyes fell. "I have only to wear a cap and bells to fit the role," she muttered ruefully.

"Come now, ma'am, don't exaggerate," he said. "Though you must admit that you did jump to a foolish conclusion about your cousin Deirdre and me."

She sighed. "Yes, I did."

"I certainly gave you enough opportunities to reconsider," he pointed out gently.

"Yes, now that I think of it, you did. *In the game of love, I am not a participant,* that's what you said, didn't you? I am a fool."

If she expected him to object, she was doomed to disappointment. "Well," he said thoughtfully, "you do seem to rush to conclusions, much as in the old saying."

"That fools rush in where angels fear to tread? Thank you sir, for the compliment." She turned away in anger and started up the stairs. She'd only gone a few steps when she paused. "I suppose," she said, looking back at him, "that's what you meant when you said, earlier this evening, that my character is consistent. You meant that I'm consistently foolish."

"Actually, I didn't mean that at all." He came up beside her. "I was thinking that you are consistently . . . er . . . closed-minded."

Disgusted, she renewed her climb. "You, sir," she threw over her shoulder, "are the foolish one if you think being closed-minded is a less-offensive description of my character than being foolish."

"I'm dreadfully sorry. I had no wish to offend." Smiling, he caught up with her again and took her hand. "I realize that closed-mindedness can't possibly be a fully accurate description of your character. I know there's much more to you than that. I hope, in the next few days, to have the opportunity to discover some of the many other facets of your nature."

"Do you, indeed?" She peered up at his face suspiciously. Was this the rake at work? "Tell me, my lord, why do you wish further exploration of a character you've already decided is foolishly closed-minded?"

"Because, ma'am, I've already seen signs in you of a very appealing charm."

Her brows rose in scorn. "Really, my lord, that was beneath you. There have been no signs of 'charm' in any of our encounters. Do you think this sort of obvious, insincere flattery will win my approbation?"

"When you know me better, ma'am, you'll learn that I never offer Spanish coin. Flattery is not one of my gifts. And even you will admit that you've shown me one quite obvious charm." The ironic gleam in his eyes reappeared. "A man always finds a woman charming when he believes she admires him."

She gaped in offended astonishment. "Are you saying you think I *admire* you?"

"Well, yes, of course. You must."

"How can you possibly believe that? I've barely been civil to you."

"But you believed, with no proof whatsoever, that I was the man your cousin Deirdre fell in love with," he explained calmly. "You couldn't have believed that if you'd found me odious."

That, of course, was quite true; she'd found him anything but odious. But it was the last thing she wanted him to know. She had no choice but to deny it. Vehemently. "Oh, yes, I could!" she declared. "I thought the girl was besotted to have wanted you. Crazed. Utterly blind. So there!"

He dropped her hand and took a backward step. "Heavens," he said. "I'm crushed."

He was mocking her, but she ignored it. "Not so charming now, am I?" she asked triumphantly.

"No," he agreed, "not very."

"And now that you've determined I'm foolish, consistently closed-minded, lacking in charm, and as arrogant as the girl in the Persian shawl, I suspect that you've discovered enough facets in my character to give up searching for more."

He rubbed his chin ruefully. "You've certainly made the prospect appear discouraging."

"Good, then. You'll give it up." She turned on her heel and marched up the remaining stairs. "Good night, my lord."

"Good night, Miss Rendell," he said. This time, he did not follow her.

The feeling that she'd somehow triumphed in the verbal battle lasted until she'd shut the door of her room. Then, abruptly, the feeling died. *What on earth do I have to feel triumphant about?* she asked herself. *What did I actually win in that exchange?* Nothing at all, if one thought about it. In truth, she'd lost. She'd merely succeeded in convincing the most attractive man she'd ever met that she was unworthy of his attention! The more she remembered about the conversation on the stairs, the more miserable she felt. She *was* a fool!

She threw herself on the bed and buried her head in the pillows. When had she become so *stupid?* Tears of humiliation flowed from her eyes and began to drip onto the bed linen. She'd never considered herself to be the weepy sort, but she realized she was about to indulge in something more than mere tears: A bout of hearty sobs was coming on. Before the sobs actually developed, however, a knock sounded at the door. "G-Go away, Megan," she ordered, choked.

"It's not Megan," came Lord Ainsworth's voice.

The intended sobs froze in her chest. With a pounding pulse and shaking knees, she got to her feet, took a quick swipe at her cheeks with the back of her hand, drew in a deep breath, and stumbled to the door.

She opened it just a crack. "Lord Ainsworth, what on earth—?"

He cut her off with a wave of his hand. "Don't you think it's time you began to call me Harry? This excessive formality makes it very difficult for me to speak freely."

"I hadn't noticed that you'd had the least difficulty in speaking freely. However, if you wish it, I shall call you Harry from now on."

"Thank you, ma'am."

"And you may call me Kate. Your insistent 'ma'am' makes me feel ninety years old."

"It will be my pleasure, Kate," he said, grinning as if he'd won a match.

"But that's not why you knocked at my door, is it?" she asked, frowning at him to quell his saucy grin. "What do you wish to speak so freely about?"

"I just want to clarify one point," he said, "to keep you from making another wrong assumption about me."

"Oh?" She opened the door a bit wider. "What assumption is that?"

"The assumption that I'm going to give up on exploring other facets of your character. I have no intention of giving up on you, Kate."

She could feel a little bubble of relief ease the tension in her chest, but she had no intention of letting him see it. She raised her eyebrows haughtily. "Really, my lord? I don't see why—"

" 'Harry,' please, not 'my lord.' " he reminded her.

"Harry, then. By whatever name I call you, the facts don't change. I don't see why you claim to be interested in exploring my character when you obviously find so much fault with it."

His eyes took on their disconcerting twinkle. "You see, Kate, my dear," he explained, "there's one thing about you that makes the exploration too tempting for me to resist."

"And what is that, may I ask?"

"Your mouth."

"My mouth?" Her heart gave a little leap, though she had no idea why. "The mouth with the arrogant twist? As in the painting?"

His grin widened. "Yes, that very mouth. It may have an arrogant twist, but it's also the most kissable mouth I've ever seen. Good night, ma'am." And with that, he sauntered off down the hall.

"Good night, *Kate*," she corrected, hoping he would not hear the catch in her voice. But he was already out of earshot.

TEN

❧

Harry turned the knob of his bedroom door carefully. He was sharing the room with his brother and did not want to wake the boy. But when his eyes adjusted to the darkness, he saw a dark figure standing at the window, faintly outlined by the light of the moon. "Benjy?" His voice clearly showed his disapproval. "What are you doing still up at this late hour?"

"I might ask the same of you," the boy retorted.

"No, you might not," Harry said, mockingly stern. "You're half my age and, therefore, only entitled to half my privileges." He crossed the room to his brother. "Is something troubling you, boy?"

"No, not at all. I was just standing here admiring the way the garden looks in the moonlight. Look at that bush over there, Harry. Doesn't it look like the Longwitton Dragon?"

"The Longwitton Dragon?"

"In that story you used to tell me when I was a child."

"Oh, yes," Harry said, smiling, "I remember."

Benjy pointed eagerly toward their left. "Look there, alongside the little well."

Harry looked. "Yes, yes, I *see!* That bush *does* resemble the dragon."

"Just like in the story, with his tail wrapped round that tree and—"

"—and its tongue in the well. Remarkable!" Harry put an arm about the boy's good shoulder, and the two stood looking out at the moon-shadowed shapes, grinning at their shared old memories.

After a while, Harry's smile faded. "You're not having a very pleasant time here, are you?" he asked sympathetically.

"I wasn't, but all that's changed," the boy said with a twinkle. "I have an assignation."

"Have you, indeed?" Harry eyed him suspiciously. "You're not going to tell me you're indulging in a flirtation with a housemaid?"

"Oh, much better than that!" Benjy said, chortling with satisfaction.

This caused Harry to drop his arm, march over to the night-table, and light the candle that stood ready. He studied his brother in its light. "Well, at least you're already in your nightshirt." He brought the candle close to his brother's face. Benjy was grinning widely. "Come now, boy," Harry demanded, "what mischief are you up to?"

"No mischief at all. A certain lady suggested an

assignation. Is there anything wrong with that?"

"I haven't enough information to tell. What lady?"

"Only the prettiest lady in the house. In the whole county, if I'm a judge."

Harry's brows knit. "You've an 'assignation' with Deirdre?"

This took Benjy by surprise. "Do you find Deirdre the prettiest?"

"Yes, of course. Don't you?"

"No, I don't. Deirdre is lovely, I grant, but my lady puts her in the shade."

Harry suddenly gasped. "Good God! You're not thinking of . . . dash it, Benjy, are you saying you've an assignation with *Kate Rendell?*"

"Well, you needn't look at me as if I planned to grapple her under the stairs!" Benjy said in annoyance. "It's only an appointment for a game of cards."

"Of course," Harry said, feeling foolish. "I suspected as much. Grapple her under the stairs, indeed!"

"I wouldn't grapple a housemaid under the stairs, much less someone like Kate," the boy muttered, throwing himself on his bed in disgust.

"Alright, enough!" his brother said, laughing and tossing a pillow at him. "Go on your 'assignation' with Kate, with my blessing."

"I don't need your blasted blessing," Benjy said.

Harry sat down on his bed and began to pull off his boots. "You have it anyway," he replied mildly. "I'm glad she's managed to cheer you up."

"So am I." Benjy sat up and looked over at his

brother. "Did you see how she had me escort her into dinner?"

"Yes, I did."

Benjy sank back against his pillow. "She likes me," he said, a beatific smile lighting his face.

I wish she liked me, his brother thought, yanking off his second boot. Aloud, he only said, "In the game of love, old man, appearances are deceiving."

Some minutes later, when Harry was under his covers and the candle blown out, Benjy's voice came to him in the darkness. "Seriously, Harry, don't you think Kate is *something like?*"

"Yes, I do," he answered. "She is certainly something like!"

ELEVEN

Benjy was waiting for Kate in the library at the appointed time the next morning. It was a good while after the gentlemen had left for their shooting expedition but before any of the ladies had come down to breakfast. Benjy, bright-eyed and eager, had already set up the card table, so Kate, wasting no time with greetings, sat down and began to play. By the time most of the ladies had come down, Kate had lost all her coins and was forced to write vowels. Benjy was evidently as wizard at ecarte as he claimed to be at loo.

At mid-morning Deirdre discovered them and asked to watch the play. "Now that there are three of us," Benjy suggested eagerly, "we can play copper loo."

"Oh, no, indeed," Deirdre objected. "You're just a boy! Much too young for such gambling games."

Benjy didn't argue but merely dealt the cards for

another round of ecarte with Kate, which, with a bra-
vura show of expertise, he quickly won. After she paid
up, Kate looked up at Deirdre with a twinkle. "Do sit
down for copper loo, my love. I think he's old enough
now."

Both the ladies were no match for Benjy, who
quickly amassed a sizeable pile of pennies from Deirdre and more notes from Kate. "You, my boy, will
grow up to be a cardsharper," Kate teased as she
signed another note.

By noon, a heavy rain was falling. The hunters, wet
and disgruntled, were forced to give up their sport and
come home. After they dried off, the older gentlemen
went to the billiard room, but Harry and Leonard went
looking for the young ladies. The sounds of voices led
them to the library, where they were eagerly welcomed
and encouraged to join in the game. Before long, the
sound of loud laughter echoed through the room. Kate
noticed that Harry's quips kept everyone in high spirits. Benjy, his eyes sparkling, seemed to have forgotten
his injury. Deirdre giggled girlishly over every witti-
cism. Leonard chortled as loudly over a good joke as
he did over a good hand. It was, Kate thought, as
pleasant a way to spend a rainy afternoon as any.

But the cheerful feeling was not destined to last.
When Deirdre failed to get a trick, Leonard counted
up the pool and announced that she owed a shilling
and four pence. "No," Kate pointed out, "she owes
only sixpence."

"Not by the rules I know," Leonard argued. "According to them, you must pay the sum of the pool."

"The rules we've been using require paying only the price of the deal," Kate insisted.

"I'm perfectly willing to abide by Leonard's rules," Deirdre offered cheerfully, reaching for her small pile of coins.

"But we're not," Kate said. "We've been playing with these rules all morning."

"But," Leonard objected, "they're children's rules."

Kate's eyebrows rose in disdain. "Yours, sir, sound like gamesters' rules."

"I suggest," Harry said to Leonard in a tone of playful warning, "that you surrender and accept Miss Rendell's rules. To insist on yours will only waste time. She's too strong-minded ever to give in."

With Benjy agreeing with a loud "Hear, hear!" and Deirdre putting a restraining hand on her lover's arm, Leonard shrugged in surrender, and the game proceeded with no further argument.

But Kate's mood was decidedly deflated. Her mind kept going over the little exchange. *Too strong-minded ever to give in*—those were Harry's exact words. Though they'd been spoken in support of her position, they could not be interpreted as flattering. They were, in fact, rather hurtful. To call someone strong-minded was not necessarily an insult, she supposed, but being described as *too* strong-minded could certainly be considered so. It was akin to being called arrogant. It was that possibility that cut her to the quick. Was she truly as arrogant as he seemed to believe? And if she were not, would it matter to his way of thinking? It seemed to her that Harry would forever think of her that way.

He seemed bent on interpreting everything she said and did in that light. And having a kissable mouth apparently made no difference to him at all.

With her cheerful mood thus destroyed, she decided she'd had enough of cards. She excused herself as soon as she could politely do so and went in search of her mother.

She found her mother in the small sitting room. Astonishingly, Mama did not have her embroidery with her. Instead, she was engaged in a seemingly flirtatious conversation with Sir Edward. Kate was taken aback. What was going on here?

She backed out of the room silently. She wanted to remain unnoticed. If Mama was indeed involved in a flirtation, Kate had no wish to interfere. In fact, she wanted to dance about the room in glee. This was just what she'd been hoping for—that Mama would find an admirer. For far too long, Isabel Rendell had occupied her days with nothing more than her everlasting embroidery. If the attentions of a gentleman, even so old-fashioned a specimen as Sir Edward Tyndale, would enliven her—even if only enough to make her forget her needlework—Kate would be the last to discourage the arrangement. And if something more should come of it, so much the better.

Out in the corridor, she wondered what to do next. She could, of course, select a book from the library and spend the afternoon reading, but the card players were there, and she did not wish to face them again. There was nothing else to do but put on a shawl and take a walk in the rain. With a discouraged sigh, she started toward the door. At the next turning, however, she collided with a gentleman in a blue coat. "Oh," she cried, stepping back, "I beg your—"

"You needn't beg my pardon," came a familiar voice. "It's only me, Percy."

"Percy!" She surprised herself at the gladness in her voice. It was the first time in years she felt pleased to see him.

He, too, was surprised. "You sound glad to see me!" he exclaimed.

"I am. When did you get here?"

"Just a little while ago. Didn't your aunt tell you I was invited?"

"Yes, she did. But I . . . I didn't know if you'd accepted."

"Oh, yes, I had every intention of coming. Though I had no intention of speaking to you. I'm still miffed at you, you know."

"But you *are* speaking to me."

"Only because you said you're glad to see me. Are you?"

She peered up at him, wondering how to respond. She had no wish to encourage him in his pursuit of her, but, on the other hand, it would not do for them to be at loggerheads during this visit. That would only give His Lordship Harry Gerard another reason to find her arrogant. If, on the other hand, he would notice Percy gazing at her adoringly during the next couple of days, it might prove to him that there were *some* people on this earth who found her loveable. "Yes, I am glad to see you," she purred, taking his arm. "I've been in dire need of some really congenial company."

An expression of beatific disbelief spread over his face. "Do you mean it? Congenial? *Me?*"

"Of course, you!" She met his beaming smile with one of her own. "Come along, now, my dear, and I'll introduce you to the others. They're playing an utterly childish version of copper loo. It will give me enormous pleasure to be able to interrupt them."

TWELVE

❧❧❧

Like Percy, guests for Saturday evening's ball began arriving on Friday afternoon. All eight guest bedrooms were occupied by the time the sun set. Two dozen guests would sit down to dine that evening. Dinner, therefore, would be an even more formal affair than the night before. The necessity to dress for the occasion brought the card game to an end by late afternoon.

Kate did not fuss over her dressing. After putting on the green brocade gown (which, she pointed out to Megan with an I-told-you-so satisfaction, would have been more appropriate for the night before, just as last night's lavender silk would have been more suitable for this evening), she decided to look in on her mother. She found her sitting at her dressing table with her widow's cap in one hand and a white ostrich plume in the other. "I'm glad you're here," Lady Isabel greeted her daughter. "I can't decide which of these to wear."

Kate did not hesitate. "The plume, Mama, by all means."

Lady Isabel threw her daughter a worried glance. "You don't think it will make me appear too . . . too . . . dashing?"

"I see nothing wrong with a bit of dash." She came up behind her mother, pulled the cap from her hand, tossed it aside, and promptly pinned the plume in place. "There! I'm sure Sir Edward will find it fetching."

"Oh! You've noticed," Lady Isabel said with a small smile, turning about on her chair to face her daughter.

"That Sir Edward admires you? Yes, I've noticed."

"You don't disapprove, do you?

"No, of course not." Kate perched on the bed and grinned at her mother. "I rather enjoy seeing you being pursued by an admirer."

"I enjoy it, too," Lady Isabel admitted. "It's been a long while since I attracted the attentions of a gentleman. I quite like the feeling of being admired."

"I hope you admire more than the feeling. It helps if you also admire the gentleman himself."

Lady Isabel shrugged. "Well, my dear, I must admit that Sir Edward Tyndale isn't quite the stuff of a lady's dreams, but then I myself am not dream material."

"You, Mama, are a very attractive woman and still in your prime," Kate insisted. "And Sir Edward appears to be a charmer."

"He's very pleasant," Lady Isabel said, "but one would wish the fellow did not still powder his hair. Don't you find it makes him seem older than sixty-one, which he claims is his age?"

"No, I don't. I thought him even younger."

Lady Isabel ignored her. "And wouldn't he seem less antiquated if he didn't bow quite so much? And if he weren't so ponderous in his manner?"

"I think, Mama, that you wouldn't be finding so many petty faults with the fellow if you didn't truly like him."

"You're right. I do like him. Besides, I have as many petty faults as he. Look at me! Swollen ankles, wrinkles about the eyes and mouth, and a waistline comparable in girth to the entire circumference of Buckinghamshire."

"Oh, pooh!" Kate laughed, jumping up and planting a fond kiss on her mother's cheek. "You know perfectly well that you look lovely."

Lady Isabel rose and studied herself in the mirror with a dubious frown. "Do I, dearest? Would you honestly say I am well preserved for a fifty-year-old?"

"Well preserved? What a dreadful phrase, Mama! What I would say is that no stranger would take you for a day over forty. So there!"

Lady Isabel snorted. "If you were any proper sort of daughter you'd have said thirty." Suddenly, her face falling, she dropped down on the little dressing-table chair again. "Oh, dear, Kate, what's come over me? Why am I being so . . . so *missish?*"

"Nerves, Mama, I suppose. Nothing but nerves."

She bent over her mother and gave her a quick embrace. "I think it's sweet that you're being missish."

"Oh, yes, very sweet! A better word would be addlepated." She turned to her daughter with an expression both anxious and self-mocking. "Do you think Edward is feeling nervous at this moment? I wonder how he'd describe me, if he and Leonard were having a conversation like this."

Kate smiled back at her fondly. "Judging from your manner these past couple of days, I think there's one word he would *not* use to describe you," she said as she made for the door.

"Oh?" her mother asked curiously. "What word is that?"

"Serene," Kate said as she sauntered out. "He would not, thank goodness, describe you as serene."

THIRTEEN

⋘⋗

The rain, still falling during dinner, did not dampen the excitement of the guests on hearing—some for the second time—the announcement of the forthcoming nuptials. By the time the men were drinking their after-dinner ports, even the weather seemed to join in the celebration. The rain stopped, and bits of moonlight could be seen edging the striated clouds. This gave Percy an opportunity to step out on the terrace to puff away at his pipe.

He was soon joined by Lord Ainsworth. "Still a bit damp out here," his lordship remarked.

"Dry enough for me," Percy responded. "I just came out to blow a cloud."

"So I see." Lord Ainsworth perched on the balustrade. "Too bad the rain didn't stop earlier. We might have gotten in some good shooting."

"Perhaps tomorrow. I'd like to join you, if I may.

Nothing I like better 'n a bit of good shooting."

"Yes, of course. Come down at six, if the weather looks promising." Harry glanced at the other man from the corner of his eye. "How's the shooting down in Suffolk? You do come from there, don't you?"

"Yes, I do. My land marches with the Rendells', you know."

"So I heard." He paused and looked down at his boots, as if he were studying their design. "Lady Madge says you and Miss Rendell were childhood sweethearts."

"Kate and I did grow up together. But I'm not sure about being sweethearts."

Harry lifted his head and raised an eyebrow. "Not sure?"

"I've been after her for years, I admit that. Everyone knows it. But Kate's not an easy girl to pin down." He removed his pipe from between his lips and threw Harry a sly smile. "Just lately, though, I've begun to have hopes . . ."

"Have you, indeed?" Harry peered at the other man interestedly. "Given you signs, has she?"

Percy expelled a plume of smoke and nodded. "Of late she has. And—would you credit it?—just as I was about to give it all up."

"Were you? Why was that?"

Percy shrugged. "I'd tried to woo her with a poem. That was a mistake." He took a last puff and tapped the bowl of his pipe on the edge of the balustrade. "Women!" he said with a rueful laugh. "I'll never understand 'em."

"But that's the greatest part of their attraction," Harry said. "We're not meant to understand them. In the game of love, women are like feats of magic—they lose their charm when we figure out how they work. Wasn't it Congreve who wrote,

'Women are like tricks of sleight of hand,
Which, to admire, we should not understand.'?"

"Hmmmph," Percy grunted. "That may be so, but how are we supposed to win 'em if we can't understand 'em? Take Kate, for example. Wouldn't you think a woman who reads poetry would be pleased at being offered a bit of verse? But no, just the opposite."

"Perhaps," Harry suggested, suppressing a grin, "it was the wrong verse."

"No verse would have been right," Percy said decidedly as he pocketed his emptied pipe. "Well, I'm ready to go back inside. Join me, old fellow?"

Harry nodded and rose from his perch. "May as well. It's too damp out here."

The two men rose and started back. "Take my advice, Ainsworth," Percy said, clapping Harry on the shoulder, "if you should decide to woo a lady, don't do it with poetry."

FOURTEEN

❧

To everyone's intense relief, the day of the ball dawned crisp and clear. All the men (including their host and Sir Edward, who hadn't joined them the last time) cheerfully went off for their delayed hunt, eager to participate in some manly action and get out of the way of the preparations for the ball. The group included an overjoyed Benjy, who'd been permitted to join them on his promise that he would ask for no other activity than to assist in reloading the firearms.

Meanwhile, the women, understanding that they should leave the public rooms clear for the staff to prepare for the evening's festivities, remained closeted in their rooms, massaging their faces with cucumber lotion and giving their abigails plenty of time to wash and dress their hair. Thus, the household staff was able to scurry about unimpeded while they prepared for the big event.

The entire staff was needed for those preparations. Chandeliers had to be lowered and dusted, hundreds of fresh candles had to be pressed into dozens of wall sconces, the furniture in the great hall had to be pushed against the walls and the carpets rolled to clear the center of the room for the dancing, and card tables had to be set up in the small, adjoining rooms. Below stairs, the French cook and his assistants busily rolled dough and minced lamb and boiled barley water and undertook the dozens of other tasks required for preparing a menu of *hors d'oeuvres* that included truffles cooked in ashes, cabbage flowers with Parmesan cheese, carrots *à la béchamel,* mushrooms *Provençal,* lobster salad on crisp orange biscuits, Chinese hermitage, oysters *au gratin, croque* with pistachio nuts, and little apple *soufflés.* The evening promised to be grand indeed.

At eight that night, the house guests, bedecked in their most elaborate finery, assembled for a light dinner. While they dined, the local gentry arrived and assembled in the ballroom. As the dinner guests began their meal, they could hear the musicians, thirty-six of them, tuning up. The sounds added to the excitement in the air.

Deirdre entered the dining room after everyone else was seated, and the first sight of her caused a chorus of gasps. She was breathtakingly lovely, her cheeks blushing pink, her gleaming hair piled atop her head with a few tendrils left free to curl about her face, and her eyes agleam with joy. In her opal-white brocaded silk gown, with its gauzy silver overdress, she was positively resplendent. Kate had never seen her look so beautiful and so happy.

Someone who did not seem happy was Benjy. Though dressed to the nines in a shiny new dinner coat and striped waistcoat, he nevertheless kept his head lowered over his plate all through the meal, never smiling at any of the pleasantries being exchanged all around him or offering a word to anyone. After dinner, Kate took him out to the hallway. "What's wrong, Benjy?" she asked. "Did something go amiss at the hunt? Didn't you enjoy it?"

"The hunt was splendid," he assured her, his face lighting up at the memory. "Harry actually let me shoot. He helped me hold up his rifle and aim for a grouse. And I hit it! Right on the mark!"

"Well, that certainly *was* splendid. Then why were you looking so blue-deviled?"

"Because Grandmama says I may not go to the ball." The excited gleam faded from his eyes. "If my mother were alive, I'm sure she would've let me stay. Grandmama is much too old-fashioned. I must go up to bed, she says. She thinks a fourteen-year-old who hasn't even learned how to dance has no place in a ballroom."

"She's right, of course," Kate said, nevertheless patting his shoulder sympathetically. "It would be terribly dull for you to stand about on the sidelines, watching the rest of us cavort about."

"Then how am I ever to learn, if I'm not permitted to watch?"

This surprised Kate. "Do you *want* to learn to

dance? I thought boys your age only wanted to learn shooting and cricket and the manly sports."

"To be honest, Kate, I'd really like to be able to dance," Benjy said, reddening. "You see, sometimes our headmaster invites the girls from the Marchmont Academy for a social evening, and several of the fellows get up and dance with 'em, but I always stand about like a dolt."

"But isn't there someone at school who can teach you?" Kate asked, touched. "One of the fellows who knows how?"

"It's embarrassing to have to ask," the boy muttered glumly as he turned and started toward the stairway.

"Wait!" Kate called after him. "I'll teach you, Benjy! It'll be great fun."

Benjy swung about eagerly. "You will? When?"

"Tonight! Why not?" She brightened as the idea grew in her mind. "Listen, Benjy, go to the library, find yourself a book, and read for a while. I must go to the ball for an hour or so, for I'm promised to Percy for a waltz and to some others for a few of the country dances; but I'll slip out as soon as I can. I'll join you in the library and teach you."

Benjy's eyes lit up. "Would you really, Kate? That'd be smashing!"

"Yes, I think it will be. If we leave the library door ajar, we'll surely be able to hear the music. And we can dance to it!"

But before her words had left her tongue, his face fell again. "No, I can't," he said, taking a backward step, "it wouldn't be right. I can't ask you to miss the ball on my account."

"Nonsense, I'd much rather dance with you in the library than with any of the dandies and prigs who'll offer to stand up with me in the ballroom."

He shook his head. "No, thanks, Kate. Grandmama would have my head if she heard I made you miss the ball."

"She won't hear it. And I promise you, word of honor, that I won't be missing anything that would give me more pleasure than dancing with you. So run along to the library and wait for me. I won't be more than an hour." And, without giving him a chance to phrase another objection, she turned on her heel and ran off.

It was, as it ought to be, Deirdre's night. After the dinner guests had joined the assemblage in the ballroom, the orchestra broke into a rousing rendition of *Rule Britannia* as Deirdre made her entrance on her father's arm. To the applause and cheers of the crowd, Charles gallantly handed her over to her betrothed for the first dance.

It was the gayest of affairs. The house glowed with lights, and the lively music, combined with sounds of laughter, rang against the high ceilings and echoed gaily in the air. Deirdre was indeed having the night of her life. She waltzed twice with her betrothed with such abandon that, each time, the others on the floor stopped to watch them. Then, besieged with partners, she danced every dance with enthusiastic gaiety, apparently enjoying every partner's companionship with equal delight.

For Kate, however, the ball was less than delightful. For one thing, she wasn't able to wear the lavender ball gown she'd intended to, having foolishly worn it before, so she was forced to wear a very pale yellow lustring with a modest décolletage and girlishly puffed sleeves. It made her feel dowdy. For another, Percy was forever at her elbow. Because she'd encouraged his attentions the day before, she had not the heart to give him a set down now. But his shirt points—the highest of any man in the room—and his tightly curled hair, arranged in plastered-down ringlets across his forehead, made him conspicuous. Dancing with him was an embarrassing ordeal.

Worst of all, she still was still smarting from Harry's unkind remark of the day before. Soon after she entered the ballroom, he came up to her and asked her to dance, but she refused him. She would have enjoyed standing up with him, but her pride did not permit it. *If he thinks me too strong-minded,* she told herself defiantly, *then let him see how right he is!* But that act of refusal gave her only the bitterest of satisfaction.

Later, Sir Edward claimed her for a country dance known as Horatio's Fancy. "Your mother refuses to stand up with me," he complained as soon as they joined hands.

"Don't take offense, Sir Edward. Mama insists that dancing is for young women only," Kate explained.

"That's deuced nonsense," he said, huffing and puffing with the strain of performing the steps. "If elderly fellows like me can do it, I don't see why—"

But Kate did not hear the rest. She was distracted by the conversation of the couple just behind her. One of the voices was Harry's. "I've heard the warning repeated often," he was saying, "that love and marriage must be regarded as two separate states. You see, in the game of love, no matter what fellow you marry, you're certain to find, on waking the next day, that he's someone else."

Deirdre's high-pitched laughter rang out. "Oh, Harry," she cried loudly enough for the people near her to turn about, "you can't cozzen me. I know that your eternal 'in the game of love' is nothing but a dreadful tease!"

The movement of the dance separated them, and Kate could hear no more. But she couldn't help mulling over Harry's words. What did he mean by them? Was he trying to warn Deirdre away from wedding the fellow who was supposed to be his good friend? Or was he only teasing, as Deirdre had said? Then a truly dreadful possibility occurred to her. *Good heavens,* she asked herself in horrified confusion, *does he want her for himself?*

FIFTEEN

～❧～

Sir Edward, having handed Kate over to her next partner, Percy Greenway, made his way back to where Isabel was seated beside a potted palm. Still puffing from the effort of dancing, he mopped his brow with a large striped handkerchief and dropped down on a chair beside her. "Your daughter dances delightfully," he announced.

"Thank you," Isabel said, keeping herself from smiling at his obvious exhaustion.

"You surely dance as well as she," Edward went on when he'd recovered his breath. "You should have stood up with me."

She felt a wave of annoyance. How long would the fellow keep harping on her refusal to dance? "I hope, Edward," she remarked, "that you are not the sort who whines when he doesn't get his way."

"Whine?" His eyebrows rose in offense. "I don't whine."

"No one believes himself to be a whiner, even if he is one," she said bluntly.

"I am *not* a whiner!" he cried. "I see nothing 'whining' about expressing disappointment at your refusal to dance with me."

She dismissed his defense with a wave of her hand. "We would have made a laughable couple."

"Why?" he demanded.

"We both look so . . . so peculiar."

"Peculiar?" He was truly puzzled. "Why do you think we'd look peculiar?"

"I because of my feathers instead of my widow's cap, trying to appear youthful. As if I could possibly appear youthful with this plump, middle-aged figure of mine. And you . . ." She hesitated.

"And I?" he urged, leaning forward.

"And you with your powdered hair and long waistcoat that's at least two decades out of date. One would think you'd never even heard of Beau Brummell."

"I've heard of him," Edward muttered. "It doesn't mean I have to dress like him."

The doors to an adjoining drawing room opened at that moment to reveal a lavish buffet. Several of the guests who were sitting on the sidelines watching the dancing rose and started to move in that direction. Thankful for an opportunity to escape from this discussion that was beginning to sound very much like a quarrel, Isabel suggested that they join the parade toward the repast.

They did not speak as they joined the buffet line with their platters. While Isabel allowed the waiters to pile up her plate with mushrooms and oysters and seafood cakes and assorted soufflés, Edward waved most of it away. He was seething. "I don't see why you want me to dress like Brummell," he muttered at last.

"All the other men dress like him," Isabel answered, taking a bite of a pistachio-nut croque.

"I don't wish to be like all other men. Besides, I've dressed like this for sixty years."

"Then it's time you changed," she said as they found places to sit at a little round table set with flowers.

He glared across the table at her. "I didn't believe, when we first became acquainted, ma'am, that you were the sort of woman who always wants to change a man—to *improve* him."

Isabel did not like his tone, or indeed, the whole tone of this conversation. "I am not any 'sort of woman.' I'm my own sort." With a deep breath, she made an attack on a seafood patty as if in preparation for an attack on her escort. "And I've yet to meet a man who didn't need improving."

"If we're speaking of improving one another," Edward riposted, determined to prove that a strong offense is the best defense, "if *I* were troubled by middle-aged plumpness, I should certainly not eat both of those lobster cakes on my plate."

That was a blow below the belt. As any woman who's the least bit overweight can tell you, there is only one way for a man to deal with a woman's plumpness, and that is to deny—vehemently!—that it exists. Nothing else that Edward could have said would have been more disastrous. Isabel, her face reddening, laid down her fork and rose slowly to her feet. "How *dare* you, sir!" she said in a voice that was dangerously low and controlled. "If you find me so objectionably plump, then I see no reason for you to seek out my companionship for another moment." She raised an arm and pointed to the doorway. "Take yourself *out of my sight!*"

Poor Edward, unable to grasp how this erstwhile-very-pleasant relationship had so suddenly and so completely degenerated, stumbled to his feet. "But Isabel," he cried, "*I* did not object to your plumpness. *You* did."

"If you didn't object to it, you would not have chosen to criticize my menu." She pointed to the door again. "Just go!"

Feeling helpless, Edward made an awkward little bow and turned to leave. But he'd only gone a few steps when he turned back. "You, ma'am, are not at all what my first impression led to me expect," he accused. "When I first met you, I thought you were . . . er . . . the word that comes to mind is *serene.*"

"I am serene," Isabel snapped back. "If I weren't, I'd have dumped the contents of this platter on your stupidly powdered head!" That said, she sat down, lifted a lobster cake on her fork, and, with a defiant glare at her antagonist, took a large bite.

SIXTEEN

After dancing for more than an hour, Kate decided she could steal out of the ballroom without any notice. But no sooner had she escaped into the hallway when Percy came up behind her. "They're playing a Congress of Vienna," he said. "Stand up with me."

"Please excuse me, Percy," she told him firmly, "but I'm weary to the bone. I'm going to slip out and go to bed."

He fixed a disapproving eye on her. "I protest, ma'am! One cannot with impunity leave a ballroom before midnight."

The formal language, contrasting with his outlandish appearance, made her giggle. "I protest, sir, that one cannot with impunity ask a young lady to stand up with you three times in one evening."

"Almack's rules," he sneered. "Seriously, Kate, no one takes those rules seriously in a private home."

"Seriously, Percy, many do. But I'm determined to go up to bed, so the question is moot. However, don't let my absence spoil the ball for you. Go back inside and press your favors elsewhere. With your talent for alamodality, no stylish female could refuse you. Try for the hand of that young thing sitting over there, for example—that vision in the burgundy-colored gown."

"Very well, I will!" he retorted, throwing up his hands in disgust. "And I'll have a very good time of it, too. Positively!" And he turned and strode back inside.

She watched from the doorway as Percy marched directly to the girl in the burgundy gown. After a short exchange, the young lady rose and took his hand. As he led her toward the dance floor, where the dancers were forming a set, he threw Kate a self-satisfied grimace over his shoulder that said more clearly than words, "So there!"

Laughing, Kate turned and went down the hall to the library.

Benjy jumped up eagerly at her entrance, and the dance lesson was under way at once. Though the boy moved awkwardly, especially because of his incapacitated arm, he soon managed to learn the basic steps of a country dance. It wasn't long before they were moving about the room in time to the music emanating from the ballroom.

"Step forward, bow, step back, turn," Kate was instructing, when a voice from the doorway interrupted them.

"Ah! So this is where you're hiding!"

"Harry!" Benjy clarioned cheerfully. "Kate's teaching me to dance."

"You might have chosen a more propitious time for it," Harry scolded. "You're making her miss the ball."

Benjy's face fell. "I know. I shouldn't have."

"Don't scold, Harry. It was I who—" Kate began.

Harry stopped her with a gesture. "Very well, I'll put off the scold until tomorrow. Meanwhile, it's off to bed with you, Benjy. You should have been there hours ago."

"Yes," the boy sighed. "I'm sorry, Kate. Good night. And thank you."

"Good night, Benjy," she answered, smiling at the boy. "We'll continue the lesson tomorrow." She threw a sarcastic glance at Harry. "After the scold, of course."

Benjy nodded and scooted out.

Harry studied Kate with a disapproving frown. "I won't scold, ma'am, if you admit that you shouldn't have permitted this," he said. "The boy had no right to coax you into missing the ball."

"He didn't coax me," she said, uncomfortably aware that she was again finding herself forced to argue with him. "I coaxed him."

"You coaxed him?"

Kate put up her chin. "Yes, I did. And being so *strong-minded* as I am, I managed to prevail."

"Come now, Kate," he said with a conciliatory smile, "there was no good reason for you to keep yourself from the ball for his sake. He had quite a full day.

I know you meant to be kind, but it wouldn't have been a tragedy for him to go to bed."

"I didn't do it to be kind. I *preferred* being here. It was no tragedy for me to miss some part of the ball." She turned away from him and sat down on an easy chair near the fire. "It hadn't occurred to me before," she said thoughtfully, staring into the dying flames, "but I believe I rather dislike balls."

"Rubbish!" Harry declared, perching on the hearth in front of her. "Every young woman I've ever met would admit to finding balls to be among her life's most significant moments—the happiest moment if she dances every dance, and the cruelest if she is left sitting beside the ferns. You, of course, have never had to sit beside the ferns, so a ball must, therefore, be a happy occasion for you."

"You must not judge all my sex by the women of your acquaintance. We are not all the same."

"But even you will admit that, in the game of love, significant things can happen at a ball." He glanced up at her curiously. "For example, Sir Percy might have found tonight's ball an appropriate place to declare himself to you."

She stiffened. "Might he, indeed? And what gave you such a far-fetched idea?"

"The man himself. Last evening on the terrace, he spoke quite freely of his feelings for you."

She felt her fingers tense. "Too freely, if you ask me," she snapped.

"Perhaps. But he led me to believe that you'd offered him some encouragement."

"Then he has obviously misinterpreted something I said or did."

"Did he?" Harry got to his feet and looked down at her. "Are you saying you do not wish for him to declare himself?"

She eyed him coldly. "I don't see why the matter should concern you."

"You don't?" With a swift, purposeful motion, he grasped her hands and pulled her to her feet. "But I've told you quite plainly that I have certain designs on you. I should not wish to pursue them, however, if you and Percy Greenway are approaching—"

She twisted her hands from his grasp. "I and Percy Greenway are not approaching anything. But as to your designs on me . . ."

"Yes?"

She dropped her eyes. "I can't remember your telling me any such thing."

"Can't you?"

"No, I can't. I only remember your declaring more than once that in the game of love, you're not a participant." She turned and walked away from him to the library table. "Besides, having 'designs' sounds so dreadfully unseemly," she said, rubbing her wrists, "that I'm sure, if you'd said such a thing, I would remember."

"I may not have used that exact phrase, but my intent was plain," he said, following her. "Having designs on a lady is not necessarily unseemly. Designs, after all, are only intentions. They may be evil, risqué, unseemly or innocent, but that's all they are—mere intentions. They mean nothing unless—or until—they are carried out."

"And you told me of such 'intentions' toward me?"

"Yes, I did." He took hold of her shoulders and made her face him. "You must remember it, ma'am. I came to your door to tell you of my designs, and you peeped out and dared me to be explicit. That's when I told you quite plainly that I had designs on your mouth."

"My m-mouth?" Either his hands on her shoulders or the words he was speaking—or both—had a disquieting effect on her. Her knees grew weak and her heart began to pound. But she could not let him see how disturbed she was. She clenched her fingers and drew herself up to her full height. "Oh, yes, I do remember," she admitted. "You said it was . . . er . . ."

"Kissable," he supplied with a leer.

"Yes, kissable." She eyed him with frank curiosity. "Is that what you mean by 'designs'?"

"Exactly."

With an air of haughty disdain, she shrugged off his hold on her. "I suppose I ought to make a show of shocked disapproval," she said, turning away, "but because, as you say, your 'designs' don't mean anything unless—and until—they are carried out, I have no need to be concerned."

"Oh, yes, you do," he said, grasping her arms and turning her back to him, "for I'm the sort who carries out his intentions." And with one quick movement, he had her in his arms.

Before she quite realized what was happening, she

found herself being very decidedly kissed. She tried at once to free herself, but his hold on her was amazingly firm. She could barely move. There seemed to be no point in struggling.

Once she ceased resisting, she began to experience an entirely new sensation. In the past, Percy and a few other young men had tried to kiss her, of course, but she'd not permitted them to complete the act. If she had, she knew it would not have felt like this. Her knees, which already had been weak, now felt as though they would give way completely. Only his arms, holding her so crushingly tight, kept her erect. She wondered if all rakes were so adept at holding a girl as Harry seemed to be. She felt her own arms, completely without direction from her whirling brain, move up over his shoulders and her hands clasp themselves behind his neck. Astoundingly, her mouth pressed itself against his as if it would never be close enough. In one small part of her brain, she wondered with a sting of alarm if he'd notice what her mouth was doing. Moreover, being clutched so tightly against him made her conscious of the pounding of her heart. She feared he would hear that, too.

All too soon, they paused for breath. Keeping both arms about her, Harry looked down at her with a disturbing gleam in his eyes. "It seems I was quite right about your mouth," he murmured.

"And I was q-quite wrong to be unconcerned!" Despite the disdain of her words, her voice was choked with her inner struggle to regain her composure.

His appealing grin made its sudden appearance.

"Are you then going to make 'a show of shocked disapproval'?"

"Yes, I am!" she declared, breaking loose from his hold, a tide of anger rising up in her.

"What will you do? Scream? Stamp your foot? Slap my face?"

"Slap your face!" she retorted promptly and lifted her hand to do so.

But he caught it by the wrist and held it fast. "Of all females," he remarked, "there is none so difficult as a strong-minded one."

In a fury, she wrenched her arm from his grasp. "Of all males," she shot back, "there is none so detestable as a rakish one." And, determined to hold on to the small satisfaction of having managed to get the last word, she stormed out of the room.

SEVENTEEN

❧

Kate closed the door of her bedroom and leaned against it, trying to catch her breath. It took a moment before she realized she was shivering. Evidently, Megan, in following her orders not to wait up, had banked the fire too early, and the room was now bone-chillingly cold. Kate couldn't be angry at the abigail, however, for Megan had thoughtfully laid out a clean, white nightdress on the bed for her and had set a candle on the table at the bedside. It wasn't Megan's fault that Kate had allowed herself to be so long delayed in the library.

She hurried to the fireplace, got down on her knees, and poked up the fire. As the flames flickered into life, she stared at them unseeing. She knew it was not the fire that was making her cheeks burn and her lips feel bruised. And the fact that she was trembling all over was not entirely caused by the chill of the room. The encounter with Harry had shaken her to the core. Troubled, she sat back on her heels and asked herself why she was still trembling over so minor an incident. Why?

True, she'd been very soundly kissed, but at her age a kiss, even a sound one, should not have been so disquieting and confusing. At the advanced age of twenty-four, a woman should know how to evaluate the meaning of a kiss. She, however, was too inexperienced to make sense of it. What did it mean? Did Harry care for her, or was this the way a rake behaved with any woman who was near at hand?

She couldn't find an answer—her wishes interfered with her judgment. As soon as she told herself that the man was a rake and his kiss meant nothing, another part of her mind answered that he was too straightforward and sincere in his manner to her to be playing games. After permitting her thoughts to race round and round in this manner for a long time, she heard a distant clock strike two. *Two?* she asked herself in surprise. *How many hours have I been kneeling here?* In all this time she'd come to no conclusion. *I may as well give it up and go to bed,* she told herself.

She rose and unbuttoned her gown. *How annoying,* she thought, *that this insipid gown should be the one I was wearing for my first meaningful kiss!*

She was just slipping her nightdress over her head when she heard a hurried tapping on her door. "Kate, please, wake up!" came a voice in an urgent undertone. "I need to talk to you." It was Deirdre.

Deirdre? At this hour? Startled, Kate ran to the door

at once and threw it open. One look told her that all was not well. The girl stood in the doorway in stockinged feet, partially undressed, clutching a robe over her stays and under-drawers. With her hair half-unpinned and her eyes wide with alarm, she seemed to Kate to have suffered some sort of fright right in the midst of undressing. "Deirdre!" she cried, stepping aside to let the girl in.

Deirdre shut the door behind her and threw herself in Kate's arms. "Oh, Kate, I'm in dreadful trouble."

"My dear, what *is* it?" Kate put an arm about the trembling girl and led her to the bed. "What could have happened to so upset you so?"

Deirdre sank down and pulled Kate down beside her. "You've got to help me out of this muddle," she begged. "I don't know what to do!"

"Of course I'll help you if I can," Kate murmured soothingly, smoothing back Deirdre's tousled hair. "But, dearest, when I last saw you, not more than a few hours ago, you were glowing with happiness. The shining star of the ball. Surely nothing occurred in so short a time to spoil the occasion for you?"

Deirdre shook her head. "No, no, the ball was wonderful! Absolutely wonderful! It was only later that I realized . . ."

"Realized what?"

"That I—" She shuddered and dropped her head in her hands. "Oh, dear! How can I say it?"

"Good heavens, is it as bad as all that?"

"Worse!"

"Then just say it, Deirdre," Kate pleaded, "for

you're beginning to frighten me to death!"

The girl looked up with fearful eyes. "Please, Kate, don't think too badly of me when I tell you—"

"Of course I won't think badly of you. Just tell me."

Deirdre took a deep breath. "It's so . . . awkward. You see, when I got into bed tonight and went over in my mind all that's happened in the last few days, I began to realize, that I . . . that I . . ."

"Yes?"

"That I don't wish to wed Leonard after all."

"Deirdre!" Kate was shocked, of course, but she also felt a decided relief. Deirdre's "muddle" was probably no more serious than a case of the vapors. "That's just nonsense," she said, taking the younger woman by the shoulders and looking directly into her eyes. "What you're feeling is anticlimax. A comedown after all the excitement of the betrothal dinner and the ball."

Deirdre shook her head. "No, that's not it. Not at all."

"Prenuptial fidgets, then. Everyone has them, I hear, though perhaps not quite so soon after the announcement. But that's all this is, I'm sure of it."

"I wish it were so," Deirdre sighed. "I would be the happiest girl in the world if I thought this was only the fidgets. But it isn't true. What I feel is something else . . . something much more troublesome."

"Then what *is* it, my love? *Tell* me!"

"I don't love Leonard. That's the terrible thing I've discovered."

Kate gaped at her. "You don't *love* him? After gazing at him starry-eyed only this evening?"

"I only *imagined* I loved him. I didn't know what love really was. But now I do."

"*Now* you do?" Kate asked in confusion. "How can that be?"

"I've fallen in love with someone else."

"Someone else?" Kate was utterly bemused. "You can't be serious, Deirdre! You can't have fallen in love with someone else in a mere . . . what? . . . two hours?"

"Sometimes love happens that way," Deirdre said in a voice of awe. "All at once. Like being struck with a bolt of lightning."

"Yes, and just as unlikely." Kate couldn't help expressing her skepticism; Deirdre's words sounded so maggoty. She got up from the bed and frowned down at her troubled little cousin. "I'm sorry, Deirdre, but this all sounds too sudden and too fanciful to be real. Who on earth *is* it that you—?" But no sooner had the question left her tongue than she knew the answer. *Harry!*

"Lord Ainsworth," the girl said simply, staring down at the hands lying limply in her lap.

"Ainsworth?" Kate cried as if in disbelief, although she believed it rightly enough. "You can't mean it!"

Deirdre looked up at her with huge, pleading eyes. "I know it's a sudden change of heart. But I can't help it. Something came over me when he spoke to me so thrillingly in the library tonight."

"In the library? *Tonight?*"

"Yes, I wandered in to catch my breath after waltzing with your friend, Sir Percy, and there was Harry, sitting on the hearth staring into the fire. I sat down beside him, and we just talked and talked. I don't even know about what, though I know some of it was about love. But when I left, I felt as if I were floating on air. I came up to my room and began to undress when, suddenly, it burst on me! I was feeling love, real love, for the very first time! And I knew that I was in the deepest sort of trouble."

"Oh, Deirdre!" Kate murmured helplessly.

Deirdre heard the dismay in her voice. "You don't approve," she said. "Why? Don't you like him? He may not be as handsome as Leonard, and he's quite a bit older—past thirty, I believe—but he's so very clever and has so much charm and wit, don't you think so? And, oh, my dear, he has a way of smiling that makes a girl want to run up and embrace him on the spot!"

Kate, at a loss for words, turned away and crossed the room to the window. She was sick at heart. The image of Harry, flirting with Deirdre—for what else could it have been if he'd made her think she was in love with him?—was enough to make her feel ill. But that he could do it right after he'd kissed *her* so passionately was even worse! What sort of conscienceless wretch was he?

She leaned her forehead against the windowpane. A tree branch brushed against it. She could see glimmers of moonshine flickering behind the leaves as they rustled in the wind. She had a sudden desire to be outside, running along a moonlit lane, running swiftly away from this place, running ... running ... to where the air was clean and pure, like her white nightdress that would be fluttering behind her ...

"Kate?" Her cousin's voice cut into her reverie. "What are you thinking?"

Kate turned round. "I'm wondering if Ainsworth has been encouraging these feelings in you," she said bluntly.

"No, of course not. He's not a bounder. But I can tell that he likes me."

"How can you tell?"

Deirdre shrugged. "I don't know. The things he said. And something in his eyes, I suppose. Or that smile. And he's always making jokes about the difficulties of marriage, as if he didn't want me to do it."

Kate came back and sat down beside her. "Has he kissed you?"

Deirdre was shocked. "Kissed me? Of course not! What do you take him for?"

"I take him for the rake he is," Kate said.

"Rake?" Deirdre was shocked. "Do you think he's a rake?"

"Mama says he has that reputation. She mentioned two ladies at least whose hearts he broke."

"I won't believe that sort of gossip."

Kate rubbed the bridge of her nose with fingers that shook. It was probable that Deirdre was merely suffering from a girlish infatuation, but the timing of it was unfortunate. So close on the heels of the celebrations, a termination of the betrothal would be an emotional disaster, not only for Leonard but for both families. It was necessary to make Deirdre face the problem with some degree of sense. "Look here, Deirdre," she said, squaring her shoulders and speaking firmly, "if you believe you truly love Lord Ainsworth, and that he has a *tendre* for you, what are you going to do about your betrothal?"

"That's just it!" Deirdre moaned. "I don't know what to do. I don't wish to hurt Leonard. After all, he's so very sweet and kind. But I ought to be honest with him, oughtn't I? I owe it to him to tell him the truth."

"Tell him what truth?"

"That I love another."

Kate eyed her with reproach. "That you love his best friend?"

Deirdre winced. "Y-yes."

"I think that would cause him a great deal of pain, don't you?"

"Yes, but—"

"And for what? Your feelings toward Ainsworth are too new for you to be absolutely sure. And you can't be sure of his feelings for you, either."

"I'm sure of mine."

"Listen to me, my love," Kate said gently, "even if you believe at this moment that your feelings are real and are returned, the fact that you've changed so abruptly proves that these matters can be unstable. Is there any harm in waiting? Given time, these questions may be resolved on their own. If you do anything now, just think of the chaos that will result. The hue and cry set up by Leonard's family . . . by your parents . . . and the house full of guests . . ."

"Yes," Deirdre said with a sob. "I've thought of nothing else."

"But if you wait," Kate pursued, "your feelings will become clearer. They'll either grow or fade. And Ainsworth's, too, may become more plain. Then, if the circumstances call for it, you can withdraw from your attachment to Leonard slowly, giving him a less-shocking blow. You needn't rush into anything, you know. You're only nineteen, after all. You've plenty of time ahead of you."

Deirdre sat silently for a few moments, digesting what Kate had said. Then she lifted her head. "You're right, Kate. I won't say anything for a while. I can hold back for a few days, until the guests leave and things quiet down. As you say, I've plenty of time." She threw her arms about her older cousin. "Thank you, Kate. You're such a dear. I feel a great deal better now."

But Kate did not feel better. If anything, she felt a great deal worse. Later, lying sleepless in her bed, she heard Deirdre's last words ringing in her ears: *I can hold back for a few days*. Kate had hoped she'd hold back a few *months*. If a family crisis had been averted, it was only temporarily.

And as for her personal crisis, that hadn't been averted at all. She could still feel Harry's kiss in the tingle of her lips and the pounding of her pulse. She kept asking herself what it all meant. What was the fellow up to? Was he purposely stirring up trouble?

Did he truly care for Deirdre, as she seemed to believe? And if he *did* care for her, what was he doing kissing someone else in the library in such a libertinish fashion? Whatever his answers might be, however, they could not change what she wanted most at this moment—to wring the blasted bounder's neck!

EIGHTEEN

✧∽

"Blast you, Kate, I'd like to wring your neck!" were the very words with which Harry greeted her the next day.

She couldn't believe her ears. That the urge toward neck-wringing was completely mutual made her want to laugh. Or to explode in fury. She didn't know which reaction would be more satisfying.

It had been a strange morning. An atmosphere of confusion permeated the household. Things seemed to be at sixes and sevens. The remains of the celebration had not yet been completely cleared away, but the staff was overburdened with more urgent tasks. Because many of the celebrants of the night before were sleeping late while others were taking their leave, the servants were required to supply breakfast to some, to assist others with their baggage, and to run upstairs and down carrying pails of hot water or freshly ironed clothes or chamber pots for the rest.

When Kate had come downstairs for breakfast, still distressed from the revelations of the night before, she'd found several things to distress her even further. For one, she was handed a note from Percy that, amusing though it was, she found quite irritating. It read:

> *My dear Kate, I write only to say au revoir.*
> *I've been invited to stay in London with the*
> *family of the young lady with whom you urged*
> *me to dance last night. I accepted the*
> *invitation, because said young lady showed*
> *more pleasure in my company than you ever*
> *do.*
>
> *I remain, although not as ever yours,*
> *P. Greenway, Esq.*

Even more distressing, she found her mother sitting in a corner of the small drawing room with her embroidery frame in front of her and her needle in her hand. It was the first time since their arrival that her mother had resorted to needlework. Something must have upset the happy state of mind her mother had shown only yesterday. "What's wrong, Mama?" she'd asked.

"Nothing at all," her mother had answered, not looking up but continuing to jab her needle into the fabric with vicious precision.

"Where is Sir Edward?" Kate persisted.

"Why do you ask me?" was the tart reply. "Am I the old fool's keeper?"

Old fool, was he? That description did not bode well for what Kate had hoped was a budding romance. She felt a sharp disappointment. She liked Sir Edward, even with his antiquated manners and his powdered hair. It was too bad her mother didn't. "Why do you call him an old fool?" she asked.

Isabel looked up from her needlework only long enough to indicate by a forbidding frown that she would brook no further inquiries. Kate, heartsick at this ending to what had seemed so promising, had no choice but to drop the matter and leave the room.

In the breakfast room, she'd brightened up a bit when she found Leonard and Deirdre sitting together at the breakfast table. Behind them, the pale November sunshine filtered in from the tall windows and painted them in glowing silhouette. They made a lovely sight. Kate threw Deirdre a happy, questioning look, but the expression in Deirdre's answering glance said as clearly as words that, although she was here with her betrothed, she hadn't changed the feelings she'd expressed the night before. Kate's heart sank again. She could only be thankful that Deirdre had apparently done nothing drastic . . . yet.

Then Benjy had bounded in with the liveliness of a puppy, eager for Kate to continue the dancing lesson of the night before. "Not right now, Benjy," she'd said to him. "It's low tide with me this morning, I'm afraid. Perhaps Deirdre will teach you." And she'd left the room, picked up a shawl, and set off for a brisk walk round the grounds.

It was about an hour later, when she was returning, that she'd become aware of footsteps behind her and heard Harry's uncivil greeting. "Wring *my* neck?" she asked with that combination of laughter and fury. "It's yours that ought to be wrung! What dreadful thing have *I* done?"

"What you've done, ma'am," Harry said, falling in step beside her, "is broken my poor brother's heart."

Kate stopped in her tracks. "What nonsense is this?"

"It's not nonsense. He's adored you, you know, since the day you arrived and let him escort you in to dinner."

"You can't be serious. Adored me?"

"Utterly and completely."

Kate uttered a scornful laugh. "What a ridiculous exaggeration. The boy's fourteen! I'm ten years older than he. At worst what you're describing is a school-boy infatuation."

"I'm not exaggerating," Harry insisted. "In the game of love, a schoolboy infatuation can be very painful, especially if the object of the infatuation is as cruel and heartless as you."

"Cruel and heartless?" Kate gaped at him in disbelief. "What did I *do*?"

"You broke your promise."

She put a hand to her forehead in bewilderment. "Promise?"

"To continue the dancing lesson. Not only did you put him off, you foisted him on to Deirdre."

He was right about that much, Kate admitted to herself. "Yes, I did, didn't I?" she said thoughtfully as they resumed walking. "I had no idea it meant so much to him. If I hurt him, I'm sorry. But I was too blue-deviled for dancing this morning."

"That's no excuse," Harry said. "To encourage his affections by being so kind to him, and then cutting him to the quick because your mood had changed is, as I said, cruel and heartless."

Kate shook off the accusation with a wave of her hand. "You're making too much of a small matter."

"My dear girl, in the game of love—"

"Harry Gerard!" she snapped. "If you utter the words 'in the game of love' *once more*—!"

His eyes widened in surprise. "I say it often, do I?"

"Only with the frequency of a parson giving a blessing."

"Oh," he said, rubbing his chin ruefully. "Sorry."

"But in the matter of Benjy," she said, returning to the subject of her own embarrassment in order not to prolong his, "perhaps I *am* at fault. I'll make amends, truly I will."

"How?" Harry wanted to know.

She thought for a moment. "I know. I'll give him that dancing lesson, but I'll behave with such dancing-master formality that he'll wonder what he ever saw in so elderly and dull a person as I. I hope that will settle the matter."

"As simple as that, eh?" he asked dubiously.

"Yes, as simple as that." And, having no other solution to offer, she started down the path away from him.

"I might have expected you to salve your conscience so easily," he remarked to her retreating back. "With your stubborn mind, you're not likely to face the extent of your blame."

"*Blame?*" She wheeled about in a fury. "For what am I to blame? You can't believe that I *encouraged* him to become infatuated with me!"

"Yes, I can," he argued, though his voice was gentle. "I believe you felt sorry for his loneliness and used your charm to cheer him. Therefore, though your motives were generous, the end result—"

"Used my *charm?*" She laughed bitterly. "I didn't think you believed I had any!"

Harry's slow smile made an appearance at last. "After last night, you know perfectly well how charming I find you."

Though his words and that smile disconcerted her, they were not enough to calm her fury. "Those, sir, are the words of a practiced flirt," she accused, "and quite beside the point. Are you suggesting that I purposely tried to *flirt* with Benjy?"

"You may not have seen it that way, but that's what it was."

"That's ridiculous!" The idea that he could accuse her of flirting with a fourteen-year-old boy positively enraged her. "How can you even *think* such a thing?" she cried. "You, of all people, blaming me for Benjy's calf love, when you yourself—!" Abruptly, with a sudden sting of guilt, she stopped herself.

Harry's eyes narrowed with sudden, sharp attention. "I myself?"

"Yes, you yourself!" She knew she was on forbidden ground, but her anger seemed to have gained control of her tongue. "Blaming me is just as ridiculous as if I blamed you for encouraging Deirdre—" As soon as she said the name, she stopped herself again. She could not throw that accusation at him without violating Deirdre's confidence. She hoped she hadn't gone too far.

But Harry had heard enough. "Encouraged Deirdre to what?' he asked.

"Nothing. I didn't mean any—"

"Yes, you did. It's not nothing. I can see an accusation in those speaking eyes of yours."

"No, please, it *is* nothing. I ... er ... I must go." And she started off again.

But he caught her arm and made her face him. "You said something when I first came upon you. Something about it being I who ought to have my neck wrung. What did you mean?"

"I didn't mean anything," she insisted.

"You mentioned Deirdre. Have I done something unkind to Deirdre? Is that what you meant?"

"No! Please, Harry, let me go."

But he would not release her. "You must have meant *something* if you wanted to wring my neck." He grasped her shoulders and peered down at her, sincerely troubled. "See here, Kate, if I've committed some offense, I'd like to be made aware of it, so that I may make amends."

She tried to harden herself against his appealingly worried eyes. "It is too late for amends."

"Come now, whatever I've done can't be as bad as that. If you can make amends with Benjy so easily, I surely can do so with Deirdre."

That infuriated her again. "How can you possibly believe that a boy's infatuation can compare with that of someone like Deirdre?"

The moment the name left her tongue she knew that this time she had gone too far.

He stared at her, her meaning slowly dawning on him. "Dash it all, woman, are you saying that Deirdre is . . . that she's infatuated with *me?*"

"Dash it all, sir," Kate echoed, turning away in shame, "I didn't mean to be saying it, but yes, that is what I implied!"

"You must be mistaken. She finds Leonard a prince among men!"

"That was yesterday," Kate said, turning back to him. "Today, *you're* the prince among men."

"How can that be?" he asked in disbelief. "There's never been an intimate word exchanged between us."

"Never? Not even last night in the library, when you and she 'talked and talked'? Something about love, I believe."

"It was a completely innocuous conversation," Harry said, his eyes clouded with innocent confusion. "About generalities. My 'in the game of love' pomposities. Trivial nonsense. She cannot have taken it seriously."

Kate eyed him in amazement. "Do you know, my lord, I think you sincerely believe that to be true! I suppose when a man is a rake, his flirtatious manner is so habitual that he uses his charm without realizing he's doing it."

"A rake?" His voice rose in offense. "Do you really think I'm a rake?"

"Everyone thinks it," she said bluntly. "Your reputation is universally known."

"I? Harry Gerard? I'm reputed to be a rake?"

"Universally."

"That's monstrous!" He clenched his fists in fury. "I've never heard such scurrilous drivel in all my life!"

"It's not scurrilous," she said. "It's widely known that Beatrice Hibbert gave up an earl for you. And that you caused a certain Miss Landers to go into a decline."

An expression of utter scorn came over his face. "Miss Hibbert, I'll have you know, gave up an earl to marry Harry Gaddis, not Harry Gerard. And she's been happily wed to said Harry Gaddis these past six months.

"Oh."

"And as for Miss Landers, I've never met the lady."

"Lady Elinor Landers' second daughter?"

"Sorry. Not among my acquaintance."

She dropped her eyes from his, her self-assurance shaken. Had her mother's gossip sources been misinformed? Was she making a fool of herself with him again? She walked away from him down the path to a dusty garden seat and sank down upon it. *What,* she asked herself, *do I say now?*

He came up to her. "Well, ma'am," he said, as if reading her mind, "what do you say now?"

Whatever her doubts, she was not one to change her mind easily. She looked up at him, her mouth tightening. "I'm not privvy to London gossip," she said with her usual firmness. "If I've been mistaken about two particular instances, that does not mean I'm mistaken about everything. A reputation such as yours does not come from nothing."

With his eyes fixed on her face, he emitted a slow, deep sigh. "I suppose, after last night, there's nothing I can say in my defense to convince you that you've misjudged me."

"No, nothing."

"Damnation, woman, if you think that last night was typical of the way I behave with women, you've very much mistaken your man."

She did not want to dwell on last night. "Whether or not I'm mistaken, my lord, does not alter the need to deal with the matter of Deirdre."

"So we are back to 'my lord,' are we?" he snapped. "Well, *ma'am*, I don't believe there *is* a problem with Deirdre. With your conviction that I'm a rake who accosts innocent ladies and kisses them against their wills, you're probably imagining it."

"It's not my imagination!" She realized it was time for the whole truth. "Deirdre told me herself that she has a *tendre* for you . . . a *tendre* strong enough to make her wish to end her betrothal."

For Harry, this was the greatest of the blows he'd been receiving. "Good God!" he muttered, dropping down on the bench beside her. He sat silently for a moment, letting the full implication of what he'd heard sink in. Then, with a sigh, he said quietly, "Then there's nothing for it but to take myself out of her sight."

"I suppose that would be best," Kate said.

"I intended to remain a few more days," he said, getting to his feet and looking down at her, "but since you, strong-minded as you are, are not likely to change your mind about my being a rake, there's no incentive . . . I may as well go. I told Grandmama to take Benjy home—out of harm's way, so to speak. Evidently I must do the same for myself." He smiled wryly. "If you'll pardon my reverting to habit, in the game of love it's good to know when to withdraw."

"I suppose it is," she said sadly.

He hesitated for a moment, as if he wanted to say something else, but then he squared his shoulders decisively. "I shall leave this afternoon."

She said nothing as he started down the path toward the house. Before he'd gone a half-dozen steps, however, she called after him, "Harry, I . . ."

He turned. "Yes?"

She looked down at the hands clasped in her lap. "Whether you're a rake or not, I'd like you to know that . . . that . . ."

"Yes?"

Despite the reddening of her cheeks, she met his

eyes. ". . . that I never said I was kissed against my will."

"Oh?" A shadow of his smile appeared at the corners of his mouth. "Thank you, ma'am," he said as he continued to walk away. "That, at least, was kind of you to say."

NINETEEN

❦

While Kate and Harry were attacking each other on the garden path, Deirdre and Leonard were sitting side-by-side at the table, lingering over their teacups in the otherwise-deserted breakfast room. Leonard noticed that Deirdre was not responding to the questions he'd been asking her. Granted, his questions were innocuous, like "Do you think it will rain?" or "Would you care to go riding this afternoon?" But the fact that she seemed not to hear them was strange. "Is something wrong, Deirdre?" he asked at last.

She blinked up at him. "Wrong? Why do you ask?"

"Because your mind seems to be elsewhere. What's troubling you?"

She picked up a spoon and stirred the air in her empty cup. "Nothing, really," she murmured without conviction.

He put a hand on hers and stayed her aimless stirring. " 'Tis not nothing, my love. I know you too well not to recognize when you're disturbed."

"Oh, Leonard!" she sighed, her eyes filling. "You are so . . . so very dear! How can I—?"

"How can you what?"

"How can I say it?"

He tensed. "Is there something you're finding hard to tell me?"

She lowered her head and nodded miserably.

"Heavens, girl, you behave as if you're about to announce that you have a fatal disease," he said, laughing to cover his unease.

"No, no, I'm quite well," she assured him.

He found her humorlessness endearing. "I thought so. You're the very picture of good health." He took her by the shoulders, forcing her to face him. "There's nothing you should fear to say to me, dearest," he assured her. "Nothing you say can make me stop loving you."

"That's just it," she groaned and burrowed her head into the curve of his shoulder. "Perhaps you *should* stop loving me."

"And pray, why should I do that?" he asked, his lips against her hair.

"Because I've been thinking . . ."

"Yes?"

Her answer was blurted out in one breath. ". . . that we should postpone our wedding."

He drew his head back in surprise. "Postpone it? But we haven't even set a date."

"I know," she said, drawing him close again, "but we'd thought about the spring."

"That's four or five months off. Are you saying that's too soon?"

The head nestled in his neck moved in a little nod.

Leonard lifted her arms from about his neck and pushed her away. "Why?" he asked, peering at her closely. "Isn't that enough time for bride-clothes and such?"

"It's not bride-clothes."

"Then what is it?"

"I think I . . . I need more time, that's all."

"Time for what?" he pressed.

"Time to . . . to be sure. To know each other. To . . . grow up."

"But I thought we *were* sure," he said, running a helpless hand through his wild red hair. "That we do know each other. That we are grown up."

She looked up at him, her large, luminous eyes wet. "But perhaps I'm not," she said softly.

He stared at her for a long, silent moment. "I know what Harry would say to this," he muttered to himself.

"What would Harry say?" Deirdre wanted to know. Leonard didn't notice the flush that accompanied the question.

"He'd say, 'In the game of love, women, like the wind, are always changing course.'"

"No, he wouldn't. I've never heard Harry say offensive things about women."

Leonard shrugged. "I meant no offense." He got up from the table and began to pace about the room before he spoke again. "Do you know what I think, Deirdre? I think the comedown after all the betrothal excitement has made you fall into the dismals. That's all this is."

Deirdre sighed. "Kate called it prenuptial fidgets."

"Did she? I wouldn't be surprised if she had the right of it." He came up behind her and stroked her hair. "But whether your feelings are called dismals or fidgets, they will pass."

She shrugged him off and jumped up. "Perhaps they will," she tossed over her shoulder as she strode to the door, "but, Leonard, I would not count on a spring wedding if I were you."

He stood staring after her, bemused. *What on earth has gotten into her?* he wondered. "Women!" he muttered to himself. "How can a bag-pudding like me be expected to make head or tail of 'em?"

TWENTY

❦

Just after luncheon, Sir Edward found his son sitting on a window seat in the east drawing room, staring out at the sun-lit landscape with so glum an expression on his face that one might suppose the rain was falling. "What's the matter with you?" he asked Leonard bluntly.

"Nothing," the usually cheerful fellow answered with a sigh. "Except that Deirdre is in a foul mood today. And Harry is leaving."

"Leaving, is he?" The older man's brows rose. "I thought he was planning to stay another sennight."

"Yes, he was, but he suddenly decided to return home."

"That's strange. Not that I blame him. I'd like to set out for home myself."

Leonard turned from the window in surprise.

"Would you? Why? I thought you were having a grand time dallying about with Lady Isabel."

Sir Edward shrugged. "So I was. But she's cast me off. Seems to prefer the company of her blasted embroidery frame to mine."

"She liked your company well enough yesterday," Leonard said. "What happened?"

"She took offense simply because I told her she oughtn't eat those greasy lobster cakes. Silly woman."

"She's not in the least silly. You, sir, if I may be permitted to say so, are always much too prone to criticize."

"I? Criticize?" Edward's plumb, already-ruddy cheeks grew redder. "It's *she* who criticizes! She's always telling me to stop powdering my hair and to wear those new-fangled trousers."

"She's right, too!" Leonard said, unmoved. "I've been trying to convince you to change your deuced old-fashioned ways for years."

Sir Edward, unwilling to pursue this too-familiar argument, returned to his earlier subject. "Be that as it may," he said, "now that the festivities are over and Isabel has lost interest in me, there's nothing here to keep me amused for another week. I think I'd like to go home, too."

"I don't blame you," Leonard sighed, rubbing his chin thoughtfully. "With Harry gone and Deirdre in the doldrums, there's nothing much for me here, either. I wonder if . . ."

Sir Edward's eyes brightened. "Are you thinking you'd like to come home with me?"

"That I am."

"Won't your betrothed object?"

"I hope so. But even if she does, I think I'll go anyway. I had the distinct impression this morning that she felt she'd been seeing too much of me. Perhaps it's not a bad idea to let the lady miss me a little." He stood up and put an arm about his father's shoulders. "Yes, sir, let's both go home."

Two floors above them, Harry tapped at his grandmother's door. Her abigail, Miss Penniman, opened it and admitted him to a bedroom disfigured by a profusion of clothing strewn about the bed and over all the chairs. The abigail, a starchy, prune-faced woman who rarely relaxed her formal manner, unbent enough to whisper in his ear as he passed her, "Take care, m'lord. She's been snappin' at everyone like an 'ungry grey'ound."

His grandmother looked up at him from her place at the foot of the bed. "I wanted to be ready to leave at noon," she grumbled as she bent over a pile of undergarments, "but everything seems in a muddle. Benjy, the dear boy, is all packed, but as you see, my packing shall probably take us until three at least."

"That's actually fortunate," Harry told her with a smile, "since it will take me that long to get ready. You see, I've decided to go home with you."

"Go home?" She straightened up and stared at him. "I thought that you are promised for another sennight."

"I've cut my stay short."

Her eyes narrowed. "But I was under the impression

that . . ." She stopped herself and turned to her abigail. "Penniman," she said, "will you please be good enough to take those hat-boxes down to the foyer?" She did not speak again until the maid had closed the door behind her. "Now," she said, perching on the bed and peering up at her grandson's face, "what is this all about?"

"It's nothing to be alarmed about. I've changed my mind about remaining, that's all." Then, responding to his grandmother's look of suspicion, he added, "Can't a fellow change his mind? You ladies do it all the time."

"Come, come, let's have none of your gammon," the old lady snapped. "You told me only this morning that you wanted to stay. And don't think I don't know why! You've been showing a decided interest in the Rendell chit."

"Have I?" He eyed his grandmother ruefully. "I didn't think it was so obvious."

"Not to the others, perhaps, but it was to me. I'm delighted, you know. She's just the sort I'd wish for you. So why take yourself home so soon?"

"Because your wishes won't wash. She won't have me."

"I don't believe it!" the old woman declared with a young woman's spirit. "She adores you. I can see it in her eyes."

"Balderdash," he retorted bluntly. "The adoration is in *your* eyes, not hers."

"Harry, don't you dare belittle my judgment! I've

had seventy-three years to perfect it. Take my word, she's smitten with you."

"I've the highest respect for your judgment, Grandmama, but in this case I'm afraid it's off." He turned away, crossed the room to her dressing table, and absently began to finger the bottles lined up on it. After a moment, he looked up and spoke to her reflection in the mirror, "She thinks I'm a rake."

Her ladyship gaped. "A rake? *You?* Impossible."

Harry gave a bitter little laugh. "Not so impossible. I seem to have that reputation. Universally."

"I've never heard anything so ridiculous."

"That's what I thought, too. But I'm told that, among other sins, I'm reputed to have sent a certain Miss Landers into a decline."

Lady Ainsworth cocked her head interestedly. "Gussie Landers? Lady Elinor's second daughter?"

Harry turned round. "Why? Do you know her?"

"Yes, slightly. And I did hear that her Gussie was ill. Can the silly child have formed an attachment to you?"

"Of course not! I don't even know her."

"Yes, you do. You danced with her at Almack's last season."

"Good God!" Harry, appalled, sank down on the dressing-table bench and covered his face with his hand.

"But the world cannot fault you for it," his grandmother said, coming up to him and putting a hand on his shoulder. "If an eighteen-year-old romantic imagines herself in love, you can't be blamed."

"Evidently some can blame me. Kate does." He shook his head in self-disgust. "I shouldn't have kissed her," he muttered.

"Kissed her?" She snatched her hand away. "You *kissed Gussie Landers?*"

"No, of course not. I kissed Kate."

"Oh." She expelled a relieved breath. "That's alright, then."

"No, it was too soon," her grandson said glumly. "Much too soon. And then there was the business about Deirdre . . ."

"What about Deirdre?"

"Nothing." His shoulders seemed to sag. "But it occurs to me, Grandmama, that . . ."

"That what?"

". . . that perhaps I *am* a rake."

That was more nonsense than the old woman was prepared to stomach. "My dear boy," she said in disgust, urging him to his feet by a push on his back, "you are nothing of the sort. But from what you've said—and what you haven't said—perhaps it *is* a good idea, for the time being, for you to come home after all."

Isabel, going down the corridor with her embroidery cart trundling along behind her, was blocked by two footmen carrying a large trunk to the stairway. She looked at them curiously as they stepped aside to let her pass. "Who's leaving?" she inquired.

"The Tyndales," one of them answered.

Isabel could not hide her surprise. "Both of them?"

"Yes, m'lady, both of 'em. They decided quite sudden-like."

"Mebbe it was the weather," the other footman offered. "It's startin' in t' sleetin' something fierce."

Her ladyship continued down the corridor in apparent calm, but she couldn't hide from herself her feeling of sharp disappointment. She went into her bedroom, slammed the door, and walked over to the window. From that vantage point she could see the goings-on below. As she watched, the two footmen placed the trunk into an old-fashioned but elegant coach with the Tyndale arms emblazoned on the doors. It was a fitting vehicle for a stodgy old fellow who powdered his hair. "Well, a good riddance, you old fool" she muttered aloud. But her hands unconsciously lifted themselves to her breast, and her fingers clenched right on the placket of her apron where her needles were stored. She was pricked by at least three of them. As she sucked away the drops of blood, a trickle of tears wet her cheeks. The tears were, of course, caused by the pain of the pinpricks, not by Sir Edward's imminent departure. At least, that's what she told herself.

Just below her, Deirdre and Kate were both gazing out of the east sitting room window, watching the sleet transform the landscape. All the tree branches and the blades of winter-browned grass were whitening with tiny balls of ice. Icicles were forming in the eaves, and with every breeze the air crackled with a sound like glass being crushed underfoot. It was amazing to Kate to see how much the landscape had transformed itself since her morning walk. A walk would be quite impossible now. Nevertheless, it was lovely to gaze out of the window at the suddenly emerging frost kingdom. Nature, Kate thought, was both cruel and beautiful.

Deirdre didn't see the beauty of it. She sat on the cushioned window seat, stared out of the frost-fogged pane at the loaded carriage, and sighed. "I suppose," she confided to Kate after a long silence, "that, if he were truly taken with me, he wouldn't go off so suddenly."

"Are you speaking of Leonard? Of course he's taken with you." She sat down beside her depressed cousin and took her hand. "He adores you."

"I'm not speaking of Leonard. It's Harry I'm thinking of."

"Oh."

"I'm quite sick at heart about him. I thought, from his manner in the library with me, that he truly cared for me."

Kate stiffened her shoulders. "I have something to confess to you, Deirdre. It's my fault that Lord Ainsworth is going home with his brother."

"What do you mean?" Deirdre asked. "How can that be?"

"I revealed to him . . ." She dropped Deirdre's hand and turned her face to the window. "I . . . I told him what you admitted to me last night."

Deirdre froze. "About my . . . my . . ."

"About your feelings for him, yes."

The color drained from Deirdre's cheeks. "But,

Kate, how could you?" she asked, utterly confused. "Surely you understood that everything I said was told to you in confidence!"

"Yes, but I couldn't help myself. He accused me, quite unfairly, of flirting with his brother. I was so furious I completely lost my head. I came back at him with a similar accusation—that he'd been flirting with you."

Deirdre could hardly believe what she was hearing. "You *said* that?" she asked in horror.

"In so many words."

"And how did he respond?" the younger girl asked, her curiosity temporarily staving off her anger. She knew she was going to be furious with her cousin about this, but she had to grasp the full story before she'd permit herself to explode.

Kate knew what Deirdre wanted to hear. If she could say that Harry's face lit up with joy, all would be forgiven. But she couldn't say it. "I'm sorry, Deirdre, but he seemed utterly astounded. He claimed to have no intention of attaching you. He decided at once to depart."

Deirdre gulped. "No intentions toward me? None?"

Kate reached for her hand again. "What could you expect, my dear?" she asked gently. "After all, Leonard is not only his cousin but his close friend."

Deirdre stared at Kate with an arrested look. "And he left to . . . to avoid me?"

"To keep from making matters worse. It was wise, don't you agree?"

"No, I don't!" Her fury now burst forth. "This is all

your fault," she cried, rounding on Kate with hands and teeth clenched. "You had no right to tell him what I told you in secret! You betrayed me! And for that, I shall never, never, forgive you as long as I live!" And she stormed out of the room.

After sitting for several minutes in stunned silence, Kate went up to her mother's bedroom. "Mama," she said, "if you don't mind, I think I'd like to go home."

Isabel nodded. "That's exactly what I was thinking," she said.

Two hours later, the sleet stopped falling. The weather was, therefore, deemed clear enough for the departing guests to take their leave. Madge and Charles stood shivering on the outside staircase as the three Ainsworths, the two Tyndales, and the two Rendells prepared to depart. All of them were going at the same time. Without warning, the once-happy hosts were being completely deserted. Though smiling and waving good-bye, they were utterly bewildered by the abrupt departure of their most desired guests.

Hurt and disappointed, they stood watching as Leonard climbed into his emblazoned coach after his father. Then Harry, after helping his grandmother and his brother into their carriage, jumped aboard without a backward look. And, finally, Kate and Isabel emerged from the house, the hoods of their cloaks clutched closely about their heads. The cold air rang with the slam of the carriage doors, the coachmen's clatter as they climbed up on their boxes, the shouts of Good-bye! Good-bye!, and the crack of whips.

Well aware of their own disappointment, the two hosts could not know of the disappointments being suffered by the passengers in all three carriages and by their own daughter, who was standing right above them in her bedroom window, weeping, with her nose pressed against the pane.

All too soon the three carriages, one after the other, lumbered off down the drive, their wheels crunching the ice pebbles coating the roadway as they disappeared into the deepening twilight.

TWENTY-ONE

❧

An icy December, a snowy January, and a wet February brought visitations to a halt. They were the most uneventful months Kate had ever endured. Her most interesting occupation during that time was reading to her mother while she stitched. Only two small incidents occurred to shake her, if only momentarily, out of her lethargy. One was a communication from Mr. Crowell on a matter of business, in which he added a postscript relating that Lord Ainsworth was still trying to track down the painting for which he'd been hunting, but he'd confided that he didn't expect it to be of the quality of the one he'd seen at Rendell Hall. The other was the delivery of a package for her mother from Sir Edward Tyndale. In it was a large skein of fine merino wool the color of old wine. The card read: *When I saw this at the Pantheon Bazaar, I thought of you. Yours, Tyndale.*

"Isn't that dear of him!" Kate exclaimed, looking at the card over her mother's shoulder.

But Isabel only snorted. "It's his way of laughing at me for always being at my needlework," she snapped. And she sent the gift back without a word to the sender.

On an unusually balmy afternoon early in March, a carriage bearing the Quigley coat of arms drew up to the entrance of Rendell Hall. Because no visitors were expected, it was several minutes before Havers, the butler, responded to the coachman's horn and opened the door.

Inside, in the drawing room, Isabel was stitching away at her embroidery frame, while Kate sat nearby reading to her from the second volume of *Tristram Shandy*. The absurd antics of the characters in the novel had kept them laughing through many hours of the winter, but Isabel was beginning to tire of it. "Here we are, approaching the end of Book Two and Tristram hasn't even been born," she was complaining as the door flew open and Deirdre burst in on them.

Kate jumped to her feet. "Deirdre!" she gasped in astonishment.

Deirdre struck a pose with arms akimbo. "What do you two mean by sitting here at the fire on this beautiful spring-like day?" she demanded before dashing across to her aunt and bestowing a quick kiss on her cheek. Then she whirled round and threw her arms about Kate.

"Heavens," Isabel cried, picking up the needlework she'd dropped at her niece's entrance, "what are you doing here, child? You didn't come all this way alone, did you?"

"No, of course not. Mama and Papa are right behind me," the girl giggled, releasing the bewildered Kate and pulling off her bonnet.

The door opened again. This time it was Havers. "Lady Madge and Lord Quigley," he announced formally, and Madge and Charles made their entrance. Madge, breathless as usual, promptly dropped her huge bulk into the nearest armchair, while Charles strode across the room and embraced his sister-in-law. "I'm happy to see we find you both well," he said.

"No thanks to you," Isabel said with a laugh. "Surprises like this can give one an attack of apoplexy! Why didn't you let us know you were coming?"

"Because we're not staying," Charles said, turning to embrace his niece.

"We've only dropped in on our way to Bath," Madge said from the depths of her chair. "We've rented a lovely, large house in Queen Square for the month."

"If you're on your way to Bath, Rendell Hall is quite a roundabout way to get there," Kate pointed out. "So surely you had a greater purpose than just dropping in."

"We're taking you with us," Deirdre clarioned excitedly.

Kate eyes lit up. "Taking us to Bath? Really?"

"Abducting you," Charles said cheerfully. "We've plenty of room, and we want you with us."

"Abducting us, indeed!" Isabel retorted promptly.

"Thank you very much, but we've no intention of going to Bath. We're perfectly comfortable here at home."

"Nonsense," Madge said firmly. She heaved herself up from the armchair and waddled across the room to her sister-in-law. "You can't prefer staying here in virtual seclusion. It's bad enough to keep yourself a recluse, but it's the outside of enough to keep your daughter hidden away. Just think, my dear, of the pleasures that await the two of you. You can meet old friends in the Pump Room—"

"—and drink the waters," Charles put in.

"—and there are all those lovely concerts at the Assembly Rooms," Madge went on.

"—and the maze at the Sydney Gardens," her husband added, "and the Theater Royal, and the Paragon and the Abbey and . . ."

While they continued to urge Isabel to change her mind, Kate pulled Deirdre aside. "I thought you weren't speaking to me," she whispered.

"Of course I'm speaking to you," Deirdre replied with a grin. "I lost my head for a while, that's all. I didn't really mean a word I said."

Kate searched her face closely. "Didn't you mean it about your feelings for Lord Ainsworth?"

Deirdre lowered her head in embarrassment. "I thought I did. Harry is so . . . so dashing. A regular out-and-outer, don't you agree? But Leonard came to see me a few weeks after you left, and he was so loving and tender that I realized I love him after all.

Really and truly love him. By the way, he and his father are going to Bath, too."

"So you're still engaged!" Kate exclaimed in relief, and the two cousins embraced warmly. Kate couldn't help wondering, however, if her delight at Deirdre's news was entirely unselfish. Despite her conviction that Harry Gerard was a rake, she found him often on her mind. And that kiss in the library remained vivid, no matter how hard she tried to banish it from her memory.

Isabel, meanwhile, was wavering. "You may be right, Madge," she said thoughtfully. "It might very well do Kate some good to move about in polite society."

"A great deal of good," Madge agreed.

"Kate," Isabel called across the room, "do you think you'd like us to go to Bath?"

Kate, envisioning a reunion between her mother and Sir Edward, smiled broadly. "More than anything!"

Isabel surrendered. "Very well, then, we'll go."

Madge clutched happily at her breast and exhaled a relieved breath.

Charles made no such signs of triumph. "Good, then," was all he said, merely adding in his most masterly voice, "tell Havers to bring us some tea. By the time we've downed it, I expect you to be packed and ready to set off!"

TWENTY-TWO

❧❀❧

It was dark when the Quigley carriage trundled into Bath, but the streets were clogged with carriages, horsemen, and pedestrians. Even at this late hour, the little city throbbed with the rumble of traffic. Windows glowed with light. They saw so many passers-by that they became convinced that the denizens of Bath never slept. When they rode past the Assembly Rooms, they found the streets clogged with well-dressed revelers. The air rang with squeals of laughter and the tinkle of music. Kate, after months of quiet country life, felt like a lonely little firefly who'd suddenly found itself bouncing among the sparkles of a firecracker. She squeezed her mother's hand in excitement.

Deirdre and she would have liked to jump down from the carriage and join in the merrymaking, but their parents would not give permission. The hour, they argued, was late, they were tired from the journey, and they still had to settle into their new abode. Good sense and a respect for moderation prevailed.

The next morning, Deirdre rose before ten, early for her. She was eager to prepare herself for an expected visit from Leonard. He'd promised to call on her and take her for a stroll through the Sydney Gardens. She dressed herself in a pale yellow, figured muslin gown with a wide blue sash tied at the back with a huge bow, the tails of which hung down like a train. When she looked at herself in the pier mirror and whirled about, the flounce of the skirt and the wide ribbons made a very satisfactory flutter. And when her maid had brushed her hair into a very enticing curl that fell over one shoulder, Deirdre was quite pleased with her appearance.

She danced downstairs to the breakfast room only to discover that there was no one there to admire her but Pruitt, the butler. He informed her that her mother and Lady Isabel had already left for the Pump Room, her father had gone to meet a friend at the Guildhall, and Miss Kate was still upstairs, unpacking. "But there is a message for you," he added, handing her a letter.

It was from Leonard, begging her pardon for not being able to keep their appointment. He and his father were delayed because of an urgent business matter and would not arrive in Bath for another two days.

Miserably disappointed, she dismissed Pruitt and sat down at the table. There was nothing to do but eat. She began absently to pick at a sweet roll when Pruitt again appeared at the door. "There's a gentleman here to see Miss Kate." he said

"Oh?" Deirdre looked up with interest. "Who is it?"

"Sir Percival Greenway."

"Percy? Here in Bath?" Deirdre's mood brightened at once. Here, at least, was someone who would appreciate her appearance. "Do send him in, Pruitt. And then, if you please, let Kate know he's here."

Pruitt admitted Percy and then marched up the stairs. When he delivered the news to Miss Kate, she did not show the same pleasure in it as Deirdre had. "Dash it all," she muttered, "must he follow me everywhere? I suppose he expects me to invite him to breakfast."

"Is that what you want me to say to him, Miss Kate?" the butler asked. "That you'll join him for breakfast?"

Kate ran a desperate hand through her tousled mop of hair. "No, I don't. But what else can I do? I wish I'd gone with Mama and Aunt Madge to the Pump Room. Then I wouldn't have to endure his company."

Pruitt studied her speculatively, his rheumy eyes lighting up. "I can tell him you went out to the Pump Room with 'em," he suggested.

Kate's eyes lit up. "Pruitt, I had no idea you were such a scamp. What a delicious, naughty idea! Yes, do go down and lie to the fellow. In fact, if there were some way I could slip out of the house and join Mama, it would almost be the truth."

The old fellow threw her a conspiratorial grin. "Well, Miss Kate, you can always take the back stairs . . ."

Down below, Deirdre invited Percy to join her at

the table. From the moment of his entrance, with the tassels of his elegant boots swinging with every stride, his stylish appearance had made a good impression on her. Now, sitting opposite him, she was studying his neckcloth. It was made of a heavy gray satin and was wound three times round his neck, then tied with a small tie at the throat. It was the most dashing neckcloth she'd ever seen. She loved the way it pushed his starched shirtpoints up tightly against his cheeks. *Why doesn't Leonard dress like that?* she asked herself. "I truly admire you, Percy," she said aloud. "You always appear so *comme il faut*."

When Pruitt again made his appearance, neither Deirdre nor Percy seemed glad of the interruption. "What is it, Pruitt?" Deirdre asked.

"Miss Kate is not at home," Pruitt said, straight-faced. "Her abigail tells me she went off to the Pump Room to her mother." And he bowed himself out.

"I'm so sorry you missed her, Percy," Deirdre said. "You must be terribly disappointed."

"Not at all," Percy assured her. "Your own company is more than any man might wish for."

"Ha!" Deirdre scoffed. "What butter sauce!"

"Not so, indeed!" Percy cried with utmost sincerity. "Surely you must know that you're the prettiest creature in all of Bath. And in that gown, with your hair over your shoulder that way, you quite take my breath away!"

"Why, Percy," Deirdre breathed, her huge blue eyes widening as she gazed at him as if she'd never seen him before, "what a lovely thing to say. You take my breath away, too."

TWENTY-THREE

❧❦❧

After tying back her mop of unruly hair and throwing a shawl over her shoulders, Kate made her way down the back stairs and out to the street. The Pump Room was only a short distance away, though an icy March wind made the walk seem longer. When she arrived there, she was surprised to see so much activity. Crowds of people were parading round a large room that seemed to Kate as high as it was wide. Sunlight slanted down from the rows of oval windows placed way up in the rafters and separated by lovely, fluted columns that decorated the walls. The height of the ceiling caused the noise of dozens of chattering voices to echo and re-echo round the room. Those who were not strolling about were sitting on the carved wooden benches, drinking the famous waters. They were, for the most part, ignoring the efforts of the eight musicians who were thrumming away enthusiastically from their places on a platform in a large recess in the wall to her right. All in all, Kate thought, it made a very lively, cheerful scene.

She could not see her mother in the melee, but she soon spied her aunt Madge sitting on a bench near the renowned Tompion clock far to her left. Madge was sipping the waters and engaging in animated conversation with someone hidden from Kate's view by her considerable bulk. Just as Kate started toward her, Aunt Madge caught a glimpse of her and gave a beckoning wave. Kate made her way through the crowd to where her aunt sat. "Kate, my love." Madge said at once, "I want you to meet Mrs. Compton, an old friend of mine."

Kate made her bow to Madge's companion, an elderly lady half her aunt's size. Mrs. Compton would have had a pleasant, unexceptional appearance except for the enormous turban she wore. Not only was its size distracting, but it was decorated at the center by a huge jeweled brooch holding one brave little feather that wiggled like a beckoning finger.

After the how-de-dos were exchanged, Kate asked if Madge had seen her mother. "Not ten minutes ago," her aunt informed her, "your mother was discovered by an old friend who greeted her with loud cries of excitement and dragged her off without so much as a by-your-leave. We've not seen her since."

"Then perhaps I should go and look for her," Kate said.

But Madge grasped her hand. "Before you leave us, my love," she said, "you must give us your opinion on a delicate matter we've been discussing."

"Oh?" Kate asked blankly.

"You see, Mrs. Compton is a friend of Lady Landers. Lady Landers' second daughter, Gussie, has become ill, and Mrs. Compton tells me it's the fault of someone we know."

Kate stiffened. She remembered the name of Gussie Landers. Her mother had told her about the young woman whom Harry had caused to go into a decline. "Oh?" she asked again, but cautiously this time.

"Yes, we were discussing poor Gussie's situation when your aunt saw you," Mrs. Compton explained, the little feather-finger of her turban trembling with every movement of her head. "We both would like to hear the point of view of a young woman like you."

Aunt Madge patted the bench beside her. "Do sit down, Kate, and give us your opinion."

Kate, feeling weak at the knees, sank down.

"The problem is," her aunt explained, "that Mrs. Compton here is convinced that Lord Ainsworth, our own dear Harry, was responsible for poor Gussie's decline. But I say that, on the contrary, the man acted out of the kindest motives."

"I don't understand," Kate murmured in helpless confusion.

Aunt Madge prepared herself for the effort of relating the details by taking a deep breath. "You see, my dear, last spring, Ainsworth was attending a ball and asked Miss Landers to dance, and—"

"You mustn't omit the most important part," Mrs. Compton cut in, leaning forward to speak to Kate over

Madge's bulk. "It is most significant that the man hadn't asked any other young lady to dance. He hadn't danced all evening, despite the fact that there were several in attendance who would have been overjoyed to dance with him. Lord Ainsworth is, after all, quite a catch."

"Is he?" Kate asked, not knowing what else to say.

"Oh, yes, my dear, decidedly so. Besides being so very charming, I believe he's said to have better than ten thousand a year."

Madge snorted. "That may be, but our dear Harry is more than that. He is a man of the highest character and morals. I shall defend that character to the death!"

"Nevertheless," Mrs. Compton said, "he deigned to dance at last with Gussie Landers. And you can be sure, Miss Kate, that the moment they stepped out on the floor, the whole room was agog."

"Agog?" Kate asked. "Just because a man asked a girl to dance?"

"Oh, yes!" Mrs. Compton insisted, the bob of her feather accenting the vigor of the bobbing of her head. "I know, for I was there. You see, after Lord Ainsworth had done nothing more than standing about all evening—without even *speaking* to any of the eager females!—he chose Gussie to dance with. *Gussie!* Don't mistake me, Miss Kate, I mean no disparagement to her. Gussie is a dear child but not blessed with any real beauty."

"I can understand that the onlookers would be agog," Madge put in, "but one can't blame Harry for that."

"Not for that, no," Mrs. Compton agreed, "but for what came later."

"What came later?" Kate asked, feeling a bit agog herself.

"Nothing," Mrs. Compton said dramatically. "That's just it! He did nothing! After making Gussie the star of the evening—for you can imagine how overwhelmed she was, with all the other girls being jealous of her and crowding about her after her dance and making such a fuss over her—he never so much as paid a call on her."

"I don't see why he should have," Madge declared firmly. "Merely asking a young lady to dance is not a contract for the gentleman to call on her later."

"Under ordinary circumstances, I would agree," Mrs. Compton said. "But in this case, with Gussie sitting behind her mama all evening like a wallflower and Ainsworth disdaining all the flirts who tried to inveigle him onto the dance floor, then walking up to Gussie, with all eyes upon him, and asking her to dance . . . well, it was far from an ordinary circumstance."

"I don't care if the circumstances *were* extraordinary," Madge said stubbornly. "It seems to me that Harry, seeing the poor girl sitting miserably on the sidelines, asked her to dance in order to be kind. It doesn't mean he was then obligated to offer for the girl! What do you think, Kate?"

"Yes, what do you think?" Mrs. Compton echoed.

Kate was taken aback. Her emotions were so confused she didn't know what to think. She needed to be alone, to make some sense of what she'd heard. She could not answer the question they were asking her, because she was asking herself the same question.

It was strange, she thought, how a simple act could lead to such complications. Harry had asked a young woman to dance. Had he raised a young woman's expectations by what could be interpreted as an innocent act, as Aunt Madge described it? Or was there an implicit promise in what he did that he failed to keep, as Mrs. Compton believed? Kate wanted to believe, like her aunt, that Gussie Landers was merely a foolish chit who'd set too great a store by Harry's kindly act, but she wasn't at all sure. Madge was making a loyal defense of a friend, but was she right?

Both ladies were looking at her expectantly. Mrs. Compton's feather-finger wagged at her as if in disapproval of her silence. But she had no idea what to say. Fortunately, at that moment, her mother arrived. Her appearance saved the day. "Kate, dearest," Isabel said, kissing her daughter in greeting, "and Madge and Mrs. Compton, too, I want you to meet Harriet Clarkson. Of course she's not Miss Clarkson now, she's Lady Tresfield. We've not seen each other since our school days, almost thirty years ago! Can you believe that after all these years she recognized me from across the room? And I knew her, too!"

In the excitement of the introductions and the reminiscences, the question Madge had wanted Kate to answer was momentarily forgotten. And to avoid having to face it again, Kate took the first opportunity to beg to be excused. "I must run over to Milsom

Street to buy a pair of evening gloves," she told her mother. "I forgot to pack them." And leaving the ladies to their lively chatter, she made a quick escape.

As she walked up Union Street toward the Milsom Street shops, however, the question of Harry's behavior churned in her mind. Even if Aunt Madge was right in judging Harry's behavior as an act of kindness, had he been selfish and unfair afterward, as Mrs. Compton claimed? After all, Kate, too, had been a victim of his thoughtlessness. Had he not kissed her in the library that night and then promptly turned and flirted with her cousin? Such behavior surely belied Aunt Madge's judgment of his character! At best, his behavior had to be considered thoughtless. At worst, the fellow could indeed be deemed a rake. Whichever he was, she could not find him admirable.

Engrossed in these troublesome thoughts, she did not notice an approaching figure until she blundered into what at first seemed to be a blue coat with bright brass buttons. Startled, she looked up past a stiff white shirtfront and a neatly folded neckcloth into the very face she'd been seeing in her mind. She would certainly have believed him to be an apparition created by her brain, except that the thud of their collision was quite real. "Har—Lord Ainsworth!" she gasped.

"Kate!" he cried, obviously delighted to have stumbled into her. "What an amazing coincidence! I was just this moment thinking of you!"

TWENTY-FOUR

❧

Kate, discomfitted beyond words by the unexpected encounter at just the wrong moment, made Harry a hasty excuse about an urgent appointment and, with the barest politeness, hurried away. If his expression showed disappointment, as she imagined it did, she didn't let herself dwell on it. According to Mrs. Compton, too many women had hopes of snaring Lord Ainsworth, what with his charm and his ten thousand a year. She would not be one of them!

But he was in Bath. And he was well acquainted with the Quigleys, which meant that he would surely come to call. She would have to face him sooner or later. But by that time, she would be more composed and better able to handle the encounter with her customary aplomb.

She needed that aplomb that very evening. Uncle Charles had arranged for the whole household to attend a concert at the Upper Rooms, where the Holzinger String Quartet would be performing Mozart. Deirdre refused to go, having arranged for Percy to escort her to the Sydney Gardens to see a fireworks display. The others, however, were all happy to attend.

They'd no sooner entered the building when they encountered Harry. Charles greeted him with boisterous affection, Madge clutched him to her bosom with motherly enthusiasm, and Isabel offered both her cheeks to be kissed. Kate, when her turn came to greet him, merely bowed. He returned the bow with equal coolness, although she noticed that he'd raised one eyebrow in understated surprise.

A few moments later he managed to draw her aside. "You ran away so quickly this morning," he said, "that I wasn't able to ask how you've gone on."

"Very well, thank you, my lord," she answered. "I take it you and Lady Ainsworth are also well?"

"Yes. Grandmama is with me here in Bath. She thinks she benefits from drinking the waters. I hope you'll call on her. She'd be pleased to see you."

"Yes, I will. But tell me, how's Benjy? Is his arm healed?"

"Yes, it is. He's back at school and delighted to be there. I think you'll be pleased to learn that he was invited by a young lady to a Christmas fête and acquitted himself quite passably on the dance floor."

She had to smile at that. "Oh, I am glad," she said. Then, regretting this lapse into friendliness, she turned away. "I see my family is moving in. I must go. Good night, my lord."

Charles, however, insisted that Harry join their party. When they took their seats, Harry, with expert subtlety, managed to acquire one right beside hers. He said nothing until the others focused their attention on the entering musicians. Then he leaned over to her. "What have I done?" he asked her quietly.

"I don't know what you mean," Kate answered, fixing her eyes on the musicians' platform.

"Yes, you do. You're behaving as if I'd poisoned your favorite chestnut mare."

"If you'd poisoned my mare," Kate retorted, "my behavior would be a great deal less restrained than this. I would have shot you on sight."

He laughed. "I believe you would, headstrong female that you are. So that means I *have* committed some infraction, but not grave enough to be shot for it. What can it be?"

"I've no notion of what you're speaking, my lord. I haven't accused you of any infraction."

"That's just what I mean. You're 'my lord'ing me again. When last we spoke at Claydon, you called me Harry quite easily and even said something very kind to me. What can possibly have happened since? In the intervening months we've not set eyes on each other, so how can I have offended you?"

"You haven't offended me at all," she said, but her manner remained cool.

"Are you saying that time and distance have turned us into strangers?" he asked, plainly hurt.

The musicians, having finished tuning up, began to

play. A lady in front of them turned her head and cast them a forbidding frown.

"I don't . . . I can't . . ." Kate whispered awkwardly.

"I know. This isn't the time or place," he whispered back. "I'll call on you."

"No!" It was almost a cry of fear. The lady in front threw back another glare.

Harry turned and stared at Kate in disbelief. "Kate! What on earth has happened between—?"

She shook her head and put her finger on her lips. He had no choice but to face front and pretend to listen to the music.

Kate was glad this troublesome exchange had come to an end, for she didn't know how to explain her behavior. It wasn't, as he'd suggested, time or distance that had made her feel cool toward him. It was her growing conviction that he was a rake. But how could she tell him that? The flaws in his character were no business of hers. Her only choice was to discourage his attentions, no matter how pleasing those attentions might be.

She would have liked to concentrate on the music. The musicians were playing a quartet called the "Dissonance," which she particularly enjoyed. Sitting there beside Harry, however, made concentration on the music impossible. The closeness of his arm on the armrest beside hers was a dreadful distraction. She tried to ignore it, but it caused a tingle along her own arm that did not diminish all evening long.

•   •   •

At the Sydney Gardens, meanwhile, the connection between Deirdre and Percy was taking quite a different direction. The fireworks display had been delightful, but soon the evening had become chilly. A wintry wind blew in, making it unpleasant to remain outdoors. To escape its bite, they started back to the house on Queen Street almost at a run. The wind whipped at Deirdre's cloak and twice sent Percy's beaver flying across the street. They arrived at the house tousled, red-cheeked, and laughing like children. Since the family was not expected back from the concert for two hours or more, Deirdre invited Percy to keep her company until they returned.

Once settled on easy chairs on opposite sides of the fire in the sitting room, Percy gazed across at Deirdre admiringly. "Even with your hair tumbled about like a gypsy's, you are the most beautiful girl I've ever seen," he said in awe. "Positively."

Deirdre put a hand up to smooth her windblown locks, trying not to smile. She knew perfectly well that it was improper to encourage such exchanges. Although she relished his compliments, she nevertheless shook her head at him. "Please, Percy," she cautioned, "you mustn't say such things to me. I might believe them."

"Believe them, my dear, believe them," he assured her. "I meant every word."

She looked over at him, wide-eyed. "Did you really?"

"How can you doubt it? Every man who catches a

mere glimpse of you wants to cast himself at your feet."

Even Deirdre could sense that he'd gone too far. "Oh, Percy, you are a silly!" she chastised, giggling.

Encouraged by her laughter, he crossed to her chair and perched on the arm. "Perhaps you'll believe me," he said softly, leaning over her, "if I admit to you that I . . ." But suddenly he hesitated.

"That you what?" she asked curiously.

He bit his lip uneasily. "That I wrote a poem about my feelings for you."

"A poem? Really?" She turned her face up to him, her eyes shining. "Can you say it for me?"

"Of course. I know it by heart."

"Then recite it, *please!*"

He took a deep breath.

> *"My love is of a birth as rare,*
> *As is for object strange and high;*
> *It was begotten by despair—"*

He paused for a moment and peered at her, but she was gazing up at him adoringly, so he went on. "*Upon impossibility.*"

"Oh, Percy," she breathed, "that's absolutely beautiful. Do go on!"

He grinned in triumphant relief. "Deirdre," he exclaimed, "of all the girls in the world, you're top-of-the-trees. Positively!"

TWENTY-FIVE

෴

Early the next morning, Deirdre, still in her night-dress, tapped on Kate's door. She received no answer, but she went in anyway. Kate was deeply asleep. Without a moment's hesitation, Deirdre gave her cousin's shoulder a determined shake. *After all,* she said to herself in self-justification, *I have something of vital importance to discuss.*

Kate stirred and slowly opened her eyes. Finding someone bending over her was startling. She gasped and sat up. "Deirdre! Wha'—?"

"I'm sorry to wake you, dearest. But I must speak to you. Urgently."

Kate rubbed her eyes. "Wha's amiss?" she mumbled thickly.

"It's about Percy." Deirdre perched on the bed and tucked her legs under her comfortably. "Mama always used to say that you and he would make a match of it."

To Kate, who was trying to shake off the cobwebs of sleep that still cluttered her mind, Deirdre's words made no sense. "Match? Percy an' I?"

"Yes. Mama knew you were holding off, but she's convinced that you'll accept him sooner or later. So I want to know if she's right. Do you intend to wed Percy one day?"

Although she now felt fully awake, Kate still could not fathom why Deirdre was asking so strange a question. "I intend no such thing, although why—and at the crack of dawn!—you would wish to discuss your mother's completely ridiculous supposition is beyond my ken."

"Because, dearest, you're like a sister to me," Deirdre said, "and I wouldn't wish to hurt you."

"Hurt me?" Kate put a hand to her forehead in utter confusion. "My brain must still be asleep. Whatever are you talking about?"

"I'm talking about Percy. You see, last night we . . . I discovered something."

"Discovered something about Percy?"

"Yes, but before I tell you, you must swear to me, on your word of honor, that you don't love him and don't wish to marry him."

"Very well, I swear," Kate said with a touch of asperity.

"I'm so glad! Because, you see, I think I do."

"You do—?"

"I wish to marry him."

Kate stared at her, agape. "I'm not awake. I couldn't be. You couldn't possible have said what I thought you said. I actually thought you said you wish to marry Percy."

"But I did," Deirdre said, grinning. "I do. I've fallen in love with him."

"With Percy? Are you speaking of *my* Percy? Sir Percival Greenway? You must be joking!"

"I'm perfectly serious. He's a charmer and all the crack. A true London beau. But you said 'my Percy.' So you do think of him as yours."

"Don't be silly. It was only a manner of speaking, in the sense of 'my' neighbor or 'my' old friend. But I never thought of marrying him. And neither should you."

"Why not, if you don't want him? Please believe me, Kate, I truly care for him. The hours we spent together last night were the most delightful I've ever spent. We laughed and talked like true kindred spirits."

Kate sighed. "Are you forgetting that you're betrothed? Have you given no thought to Leonard?"

"Of course I thought of Leonard. But Leonard doesn't speak to me the way Percy does. If only you'd heard him last night. He said the most delicious things to me."

"If memory serves," Kate said drily, "you said the same sort of things about Allsworth, a mere four months ago."

"Yes, Harry was utterly charming, I admit, but Percy . . . why, he even composed a message of his love especially for me."

"Did he, indeed?" Kate eyed her bedazzled cousin with pitying amusement. "A poem, perhaps?"

"Good gracious! How did you know?"

Kate rolled her eyes skyward. "Just a lucky guess."

"You should have heard it, Kate," Deirdre rhapsodized. "No one has ever written a poem to me before. It was the loveliest thing."

"I'm sure it was," Kate said with a helpless sigh, "but Deirdre, please don't make him any promises for at least a week."

"A whole week? But why?"

"Because, my impetuous cousin, in that time you may very likely discover someone else with whom to fall in love."

TWENTY-SIX

❦

Sir Edward and Leonard arrived in Bath just before midnight the next day. Because the hour was too advanced to make calls, Leonard merely sent a note to his friend Harry that he'd arrived and was staying in rooms on Pierrepont Street.

He was to regret that act, for Harry charged into his bedroom the next morning at the ungodly hour of eight A.M. "Wake up, you slugabed," he ordered, callously pulling off the comforter into which Leonard was snuggled.

"Wha's th' matter?" the bewildered redhead asked, sitting up in alarm.

"I have to go to Cheltenham. Want to ride with me?"

Leonard blinked. "You woke me up at dawn to ask me that?"

"It isn't dawn. The sun's been up for hours. It's after

eight. I want to be back by midnight, so get up and dress, if you're going with me."

"Well, I'm not," Leonard grumped and pulled his coverlet out of Harry's hand. "Eight o'clock's the crack of dawn to me." He wrapped himself up in the comforter and threw himself back onto the pillows.

"Very well, if you must sleep away a promising adventure," Harry said and started out.

"Adventure?" Leonard opened one eye.

"I'm going to Cheltenham to see a painting. I'm told it's in an old castle with a tower and a moat. Who knows what we may find lurking inside. It sounds just the sort of place for ghosts."

"What we'll find is a dotty old codger who'll gabble nonsense at us until our ears ache," Leonard said in disgust, nevertheless tossing aside the bedclothes and throwing his legs over the side of the bed, "and then we'll discover it's all for nothing. It won't be the painting you want."

"Probably not," Harry said complacently, "but in that diatribe I did hear the word 'we,' did I not? So you're coming?"

"Yes, you clodcrusher, I'll go with you, damme for a fool. I hope you can spare me ten minutes to dress."

Half an hour later, they were tooling along the North Road in Harry's curricle and pair, Harry handling the horses and Leonard perched on the seat beside him. "My agent sent me word that the latest painting he's discovered is a very likely candidate," Harry told his friend. "It's called *The Girl in White*, but the description mentions that she's fair-haired and wearing a blue scarf of some kind. That sounds promising, doesn't it?"

"Is the painting signed?" Leonard asked.

"No, but my noble ancestor didn't always sign his work. Family legend has it that he had high standards and didn't always approve of his own creations. If he felt a particular work fell short of his expectations, he would toss it aside unsigned."

"Then this painting will probably not be a great work of art?"

"Probably not. But Grandmama wants it because it's a family portrait and belongs in the gallery with the rest of the family portaits. She's not particularly interested in its artistic value."

"But you are?"

Harry shrugged. "I'm not expecting a great work, but I keep hoping it will reveal that the artist had some talent."

"I suppose that really talented artists are a rare breed," Leonard said thoughtfully. "Did I tell you that Charles has promised me a portrait of Deirdre as a wedding present? I hope he finds an artist who can do her justice."

Harry nodded. "I hope so, too. You wouldn't wish to have an inferior portrait forever staring down at you from above the fireplace. By the way, Leonard, when is that wedding to be?"

"That's a good question," Leonard said, rubbing his chin ruefully. "I can't get Deirdre to make up her mind. She seems very skittish of late."

"Skittish?"

"Yes. As if she weren't certain of her feelings. I sometimes suspect she enjoys flirting too much and isn't willing to give up those girlish pleasures for the more matronly ones of marriage."

"That's understandable. She's only nineteen, after all."

"Most young ladies are married by that age," Leonard argued. "By the time they're twenty, if they aren't wed, their mothers are becoming nervous, by twenty-one they're considered on the shelf, and by twenty-two they may just as well take up the spinning wheel and the spinster's cap."

"What utter nonsense!" Harry exclaimed in horror. "Isn't Deirdre's cousin twenty-four? No one could possibly think of her as a spinster. But by your standards, she could be called—good God!—an *ape leader!*"

"In Kate's case, that would be going too far, I admit. She's too attractive and independent to be called a spinster." Leonard turned round on his seat and looked at his friend through narrowed eyes. "But you, Harry Gerard, seem to have rushed to her defense with more vehemence than my ill-considered remarks warranted." The corners of his mouth twisted upward into an impish grin. "Can it be that you've more than a casual interest in the spinster in question?"

"Refer to her as a spinster just once more, you muttonhead, and I shall call you out! But to answer your question, it doesn't matter whether I've an interest in her or not. She doesn't like me above half. She thinks I'm a rake."

Leonard guffawed. "You?" he asked, choking.

Harry glared at him. "I'm not at all certain I like that response. Is the idea so ludicrous to you? Am I not debonair enough or practiced enough in coquetry to be thought of in that way?"

"No, Harry, you're not. To tell the truth, the idea *is* ludicrous. You've not a rakish instinct in your nature."

"And what, may I ask, leads you to that conclusion?" Harry asked, offended. "If I liked, I'm sure I could make my mark with the ladies with the best of the rakes."

"That's just it—if you liked. But it's not what you'd like, is it? You're not the sort to flit from woman to woman. You'd more likely set your heart on one, and you'd probably remain true to her forever."

"You make me sound a dreadful bore," Harry sighed, "but you're probably right, worse luck."

"Why worse luck?"

"Because—should I happen to set my sights on someone who doesn't want me, I'd be in a fine fix."

Leonard raised one questioning eyebrow. "Have you already set those sights on someone? Is it Kate?"

Harry shrugged. "I'm afraid so."

"Then you *are* in a fix. If she's set against you, she's not the sort to change her mind."

"Never mind. I don't despair," Harry said, snapping the reins with spirit. "I may not be a rake, but I can be as strong-minded as she. If there's a way to win that lady, I'll find it."

By mid-afternoon they'd reached Cheltenham. The castle they sought was as antiquated and musty as

Harry had promised, although their host was not as talkative as Leonard had feared. He did, however, insist that they stay to tea and meet his wife and their daughter. The daughter turned out to be a sour-faced woman well into her thirties, excessively tall and bony. She used the occasion to engage in a desperate attempt at flirtation with both visitors. Harry was sorry for her, but Leonard found her laughable. "There's a good example of what we spoke of earlier," he whispered to Harry when they had a moment alone.

"A spinster, you mean?" Harry asked.

"Worse," Leonard said. "An ape leader."

It took all of Harry's tact to bring the tea party to a conclusion and convince their host to get to the business of their visit—the painting. They were led down a long gallery to the far end, where their host unveiled the portrait in question. It was a simple work, the subject—a young girl with fair hair—placed squarely in the center, facing forward, against a background of greenery. Her white dress was covered not with a shawl but an open, half-sleeved, blue silk pelisse. "What a lovely creature!" Leonard exclaimed at his first sight of the girl.

"Yes," Harry agreed. "And it is definitely the portrait I've been seeking."

"How can you be sure?" Leonard wanted to know.

"It's that little elm tree in the corner there in the background. You can just make out the stone wall behind it. It's the wall of our rose garden. That elm has grown quite old and gnarled since, but the placement makes it recognizable."

A price for the purchase was soon agreed upon, and the two visitors, explaining that they had seven hours or more of travel ahead of them, made a quick exit. As Harry was placing the portrait in his curricle, Leonard took another look at the painted face. "She is quite lovely, don't you think so?" he asked.

"Yes, she is. I think Grandmama will be very pleased."

"You, however, are not showing particular enthusiasm," Leonard pointed out as they climbed up to their seats.

"I'm as pleased as I expected to be," Harry said, picking up the reins.

"But you don't like it as well as you did the portrait you saw at Rendell Hall."

"I didn't expect to find anything like the Rendell portrait," Harry said as he urged the horses forward. "This is a very decent work, but the Rendell portrait—" He sighed as he visualized the other work in his mind's eye. "—that one is a masterpiece."

TWENTY-SEVEN

꧁꧂

The next day word was sent to the Rendell rooms
that the Tyndales, father and son, had arrived. The
family waited all day, but the pair did not call. Charles,
urged by the females who were all a bit worried at
their unexplained absence, took himself to Pierrepont
Street. When he found Edward perfectly well, he demanded an explanation.

Sir Edward shrugged helplessly. "Harry dragged
Leonard off this morning on some mysterious errand,
and they won't be back until late. But we'll certainly
call tomorrow morning." He glanced up at Charles
with a strange look. "You'll all be home, of course?"

"Yes, of course," Charles replied. "Why do you
ask?"

Edward took a breath. "Isabel, too?" he asked.

"I suppose so," Charles said carelessly, having no

sense of the significance of the question. "Come for breakfast."

But Isabel was not at home the next morning. Having arisen early, she came downstairs to find herself completely alone. Not at all disturbed by the absence of company, she set about to do what she hadn't had a chance to do since they'd arrived—her embroidery. She'd brought her frame on wheels with her, of course, but to her dismay, she discovered that, in the confusion of the hurried packing her brother had imposed on her, she'd left her embroidery apron and her basket of threads at home. She immediately threw on a cloak and set out to Milsom Street to rectify the situation.

A well-stocked haberdashery, supplied with feminine goods like ribbons and laces as well as hats and linens for men, provided her with just the right blue thread she needed. It was a charming little shop, and she spent the better part of an hour browsing through their stock. By the time she'd finished, she'd purchased, in addition to the blue, a skein of silver silk, a breathtaking orange, a Nile green that she probably would never use, a package of needles, and, for good measure, a lovely straw basket to keep them in. With her new basket swinging from her arm, she strolled happily toward home. Just as she turned into Queen Street, she saw Sir Edward and Leonard approaching from the other direction. Politeness demanded that she stop to greet them. "Oh, blast!" she muttered in annoyance.

They came together at the front gate, and the two gentlemen lifted their hats. Isabel turned at once to the son. "Leonard," she said brightly, offering her cheek, "so you've come at last. Deirdre has been eager for your arrival." Then, as an afterthought, she turned to his father. "And Sir Edward," she said coldly, "how do you—?" She stopped short, gaping in surprise.

"I'm glad to see you," Edward said with nervous sincerity. "I've . . . er . . . missed you."

Leonard looked from one to the other, his eyes twinkling. "I'll run inside," he said. "You both may take your time."

When he'd gone, Isabel stared at Edward in frank astonishment. "You've stopped powdering your hair!" she gasped.

"Yes." He twisted his tricorne in his hands. "Do you approve?"

"Approve? I've no right to approve or disapprove. But you look at least a decade younger."

"Do I?" He smiled at her in relief. "I did it for you, you know."

"For me? Why on earth would you do it for me?" Nevertheless, she circled round him to view him from the back.

"You know why. To make amends. For offending you."

"I don't know what you're speaking of," Isabel lied.

"That day at Claydon, when I told you not to eat those greasy lobster cakes."

"I don't remember any such incident," she said icily. "And if you're going to speak nonsense, let's get out of the chill and do it inside."

She opened the gate and marched up to the door.

Edward meekly followed. As they went down the hall to the sitting room, she turned to him. "If you really wanted to make amends, you'd do more than stopping the powdering. You'd cease wearing those outmoded knee breeches and get yourself some proper trousers."

"If I do, can we then be friends again?" he asked humbly.

"Perhaps." But she softened the word with a tiny upturn of the corners of her mouth. "It might interest you to know," she said as they came up to the door, "that I've removed lobster cakes from my diet."

By the time they arrived at the sitting room door, Edward was beaming, and Isabel's eyes had a sparkle they'd not had in months. But inside, the scene that greeted their eyes caused both of them to pale. Opposite them, in front of the windows, stood Deirdre, wrapped in Percy's arms. It was plain that they'd been in a close embrace, for their faces clearly revealed their embarrassment and guilt. And just inside the doorway, Leonard was staring across at them, frozen-faced.

"L-Leonard," Deirdre was stammering, "I m-meant to t-tell you—"

"Happened out of the blue," Percy explained with a bit of a smirk. "Can't be helped, old chap. One of those things, don't you know?"

"One of those things, was it?" Leonard growled, shaking himself out of his stupor. He crossed the room in two strides, tightened a fist, and swung it sharply at Percy's chin.

Percy dropped heavily to the floor. Deirdre screamed.

"*There's* something out of the blue, 'old chap'!" Leonard sneered, rubbing his sore knuckles.

"Leonard, how could you?" Deirdre cried, wringing her hands.

"Deirdre, how could *you?*" the betrayed fellow retorted in disgust.

"You've killed him!" Deirdre knelt down and began to chafe Percy's hands. Percy stirred, groaned, and lifted his head.

"There," Leonard said. "He may even be well enough for me to knock him down again." And he pulled Percy to his feet, grasped him by his collar, and hauled him across the room. By this time, Charles and Madge, whose bedroom was directly above, had heard the commotion and come running down, alarm written on their faces. "What's been going on here?" Charles demanded, pushing past Edward and Isabel and bursting into the room.

"I'm ridding your house of a rodent," Leonard said, and shoved Percy past them, down the passage, and out the front door. Then he slammed it shut and strode back to the sitting room, a scowl darkening his round, freckled face.

"Oh, Papa," Deirdre screamed, "he's killed poor Percy!"

Edward ran to the window and peered out. "He's all right," he announced. "The damned make-bait's running off."

"Will someone please tell me what's been going on

here?" Charles demanded, turning on Leonard furiously.

Leonard glared back at him. "Your daughter can give you the details," he said. "I won't humiliate myself by reviewing them. I'll only say that she's given me adequate cause to withdraw from our betrothal. I leave it to you to make the appropriate announcement in the *Times*. And now, if Pruitt will give me back my hat, I'll take my leave."

He stalked from the room. Edward, with a longing glance at Isabel, followed. Madge, breathing heavily, ran to her daughter. "Deirdre, my dearest girl, what in heaven's name has happened?"

Deirdre covered her face with her hands. "Go away, please, Mama. Everyone, please leave me alone. I d-don't want to talk about it. Not now."

Madge peered at her helplessly. Charles, also feeling helpless, hesitated for a moment before he took his wife's arm and urged her to the door. "Come along, my love. And you, too, Isabel. Perhaps it's best to leave her alone for a bit."

As soon as Deirdre heard the door close behind them, she sank down on the nearest chair and gave way to a flood of tears. When the paroxysm subsided, she got up and began to pace about the room in aimless circles. Percy, she realized, had not shown himself to advantage in the crisis that had just occurred. His behavior had not been courageous, certainly not when measured by her standards for romantic heroes. Had she been hasty in deciding she loved him? And if she had, what had she done to her life? She was ruined, totally ruined! Unseeing, she stumbled into a wall, slid down to the floor, and, resting her head on her knees, succumbed to despair.

It was then that the butler, not hearing a sound from the sitting room and assuming it was deserted, opened the door to admit Harry. "Yes, Miss Kate is home, Lord Ainsworth," he was saying. "I'll fetch her for you."

Harry came in and, glancing about to find himself a seat, saw the huddled figure in the corner. The tousled golden hair was immediately recognizable. "Deirdre?" he asked wonderingly. "Are you hiding from someone?"

The head came up, and two blue eyes, brimming with tears, stared up into his. "Harry!" she cried. "Thank goodness you're here!"

He crossed the room to her and helped her to her feet. Before he could let her go, she flung herself into his arms. "Oh, Harry," she wept into his shoulder, "I've made such a terrible mull of everything."

Harry, startled though he was, managed to speak soothingly. "Whatever it is, Deirdre, can't possibly be as bad as that."

"Yes, it c-can," she insisted. "You said it yourself: 'In the g-game of l-love, the players wear n-no armor.'"

"Did I say that?" He shook his head in self-disgust. "You must learn not to pay any heed to my pompous pronouncements."

"I p-pay heed to everything you s-say. You're the c-cleverest p-person I know!"

"In that case, why don't you tell me about this mull you've made."

Deirdre promptly began to relate—between sobs and hiccoughs—the whole tale of this disastrous event. "And now Leonard is f-finished with m-me," she concluded, "and I shall s-s-spend my life as a dowdy s-s-spinster!"

Harry patted her head. "What nonsense. The beautiful Deirdre Quigley a spinster? That's as likely as the Regent moving himself and all the court to Timbuktu."

She lifted her head at that, the clouded blue of her eyes clearing. "Do you mean it, Harry?"

"Of course I do." He grinned down at her. "In the game of love, you'll always be a winner."

She sniffed away the last of her tears and managed a small smile. "I do believe you've lifted my spirits," she said softly. "I think, Harry, that you're the only one in the world who could."

The door opened and Kate came in. At the sight of Deirdre in Harry's arms, she stopped short. "Oh!" she said, coloring.

"Good afternoon, Kate," Harry said. "I called to see you and found your cousin in a heap on the floor, weeping."

"Indeed?"

"Didn't you hear the commotion?" Deirdre asked her.

Kate realized that there was more—and, perhaps, less—to this scene than she'd imagined at first. "What commotion?" she asked in guilty concern. "What happened, Deirdre?"

Harry released the girl. "Sit down, Deirdre, and dry your eyes. I'll take my leave and permit you tell your cousin all about it in private." He helped her into a chair and turned to Kate. "Will you see me out, ma'am?"

Kate nodded and led him from the room. In the passageway, he sighed deeply. "I suppose it's not possible for us to talk now, is it?"

"Not if Deirdre needs me," Kate said.

"Dash it all, I've wanted urgently to speak with you, but last time I was thwarted by the music, and now I'm thwarted by Deirdre's crisis. When am I to have a moment of your company?"

"How can I say?" she answered, lowering her eyes.

He took her by the shoulders. "Look at me, Kate. I'm warning you that I can be as stubborn and hardheaded as you. Will-you, nill-you, I shall find a way to see you. And soon!"

She looked up at him, expecting him to let her go, but he did not. "Good afternoon, my lord," she said pointedly.

He pulled her closer. "No, it hasn't been a good afternoon. But I can make it better."

There was a look in his eyes that she'd seen before. She remembered at once where she'd seen it—in the Claydon library on that infamous night. She stiffened. "You wouldn't—!

He smiled. "Are you sure?"

"How can I be sure?" she said icily. "I'm not familiar with the manners of a rake."

His smile died, and his eyes narrowed. "So that's

it, is it? That's what's wrong between us. You still think me a rake."

She put up her chin. "I don't think of you at all, my lord."

"Then perhaps this will keep me in your mind," he said, and putting his hands on both sides of her face, he lifted it up and roundly kissed her. He held her there until they both had no breath left. Then he dropped his hold. "As any rake would tell you," he said with a grin, "in the game of love, the rules are never fair."

Before she could catch her breath and retort, he was gone.

She tottered down the hallway, her head in a whirl. How could she have so meekly surrendered to his advances when love was merely a game to him, the rake! She was considered by everyone—and by herself—as a strong-willed woman, but she was a wilting violet whenever he was close to her. She was thoroughly ashamed of herself.

But Deirdre was waiting. Kate shook herself out of the daze his kiss had placed her in and hurried into the room. "Deirdre, my dear, what is the dreadful thing that happened to you?"

Deirdre turned to her, her face aglow with happiness. "Nothing dreadful at all," the girl breathed. "You were right about Percy. I don't love him at all. I'm in love with Harry after all."

TWENTY-EIGHT

❧

After being kept up half the night by Deirdre's over-wrought revelations, Kate decided the next morning that she needed some time alone. She could not bear to listen to more of Deirdre's effusive praises of Harry's character, appearance, wit, and charm, so she left the house right after breakfast to take a long walk. On her way out, she met Percy on his way in. The poor fellow's chin was swollen, and he'd covered a bruise on his cheekbone with thick, lead-based *maquillage* that made him look clownish. For a moment, she considered warning him that his visit with Deirdre would not be what he expected, but a second thought restrained that impulse. Her attempt to reason with Deirdre had not made the slightest impression, and reason would probably have no effect on Percy, either. So she merely said "Good morning," and walked on.

If Percy were the sort to read omens, he would have

found Pruitt's opening remarks to be a warning of bad news to come. "Miss Deirdre is still asleep," the butler informed him. "If you wish to wait, I'll tell her maid to inform her of your presence as soon as she wakes."

But Percy could not read omens. He chose to wait. He was kept waiting for more than an hour. And when Deirdre did appear, her greeting was far from meeting his expectations. She looked so delectable in a diaphanous dressing gown covered with flounces, with her hair hanging about her shoulders in enticing disarray, that he'd immediately attempted to take her in his arms, but she held him off. "Good heavens," were her first words. "What's that dreadful stuff on your face?"

"It's a cosmetic plaster," he replied sullenly. "To cover a discoloration."

"It makes you look ridiculous."

"Does it, indeed?" he snapped, offended. "And who's fault is it that I had to apply it? If you'd informed your hot-headed betrothed of our attachment as you'd promised, I wouldn't have been subjected to—"

She cut him off with a gesture. "Please sit down, Percy," she said, pointing to a chair some distance away. "I have something to tell you that I fear will cause you pain."

He eyed her suspiciously. "I'll stand, thank you. What is it now?"

"I think I've made a mistake," she said, dropping her eyes. "I don't believe I love you after all."

"How can that be?" he asked, outraged. "Only yesterday you said—"

"I know. I'm sorry, Percy. But, you see, my heart has belonged to another for a great while. You made me forget for a time, but—"

"Good God!" His hand went instinctively to his swollen chin. "You aren't going back to that pugnacious monster, Tyndale, are you?"

"No. It's someone else."

"Someone *else?*" It was almost a shout. "What sort of hubble-bubble female are you?"

She drew herself up proudly. "If you're going to be insulting, Percy Greenway, you'd better go. This conversation is over."

"It's not over! Who's the fellow who's superceded me?"

"That's none of your affair."

"It's very much my affair. After all I've been through, I deserve to know. I shan't leave till I do."

She blinked at him, nonplussed. But how else, she wondered, could she be rid of him? "Very well, if you must know," she admitted reluctantly, "it's Lord Ainsworth."

"Ainsworth? I don't believe it. He ain't in the petticoat line."

"Whether he is or not," she said coldly, "I've told you his name. Now keep your word and go."

"Very well, Miss Quigley," he said, tightlipped, "I'll go. But you ain't heard the last of me!"

Kate, meanwhile, had walked as far as the Assembly Rooms and was ready to turn back when she came face-to-face with Lady Ainsworth. Harry's grandmother, dressed somberly in black lace, looked more frail than she'd seemed at Claydon and was leaning heavily on a cane. But when she recognized Kate, her whole aspect brightened. "My dear girl!" she exclaimed with genuine pleasure, "I've been longing to see you."

"And I you," Kate said, making a bow. "I was planning to call on you this very day."

"Then this meeting is a most fortunate chance. Have you some time now? There's a rather quaint little tea-shop just round the corner on Alfred Street. Do come and have some tea with me."

Kate willingly agreed. Soon they were settled at a small table near the shop's latticed window. The conversation was politely conventional until the tea was poured and the blueberry scones served. Then Lady Ainsworth glanced over at Kate, her eyes twinkling mischievously. "My grandson tells me he's quite taken with you, my dear."

Kate shook her head. "It's nothing but a schoolboy infatuation, your ladyship. He's probably cured of it, now that he's back at school."

Lady Ainsworth laughed. "Oh, my dear, I didn't mean Benjy. I'm speaking of Harry."

Kate almost choked on a bit of scone. "Harry? Taken with me?" she managed.

"Very much so," the old woman said.

"He couldn't . . ." She felt herself redden. "He didn't tell you that, did he?"

"He didn't have to. It's plain as pikestaff." She lifted a pince-nez that was hanging from a chain round her neck, placed it on her nose, and peered at Kate through the lenses. "But you don't like him much, do you?"

Kate expelled a troubled breath. How should she answer? She couldn't lie to this perceptive, straightforward old woman whom she found so admirable. "How could I not like him?" she said, nervously crushing a piece of her scone into crumbs. "Everyone agrees that he's handsome and charming."

"But you're not everyone," Lady Ainsworth said, her tone of voice questioning.

"No, I'm not."

"Harry tells me you think him a rake."

Kate's eyes met the older woman's direct gaze. "I do have that impression," she admitted.

"You're quite wrong about him, my dear," Lady Ainsworth said firmly. "A rake is a licentious bounder who resorts to trickery and lies to get his way with women. Harry, on the other hand, is the most honest and honorable man I've ever known."

Kate smiled at her. "You're his grandmother. What else can you think of him?"

"It's true that I can't be objective about him. He is very special to me. As I am to him, no doubt, for he lost both his parents at an early age, you know."

"No, I didn't know."

Kate's obvious interest encouraged Lady Ainsworth to go on. "His mother, you see, died giving birth to Benjy. And his father died in the very same year, victim of a dreadful coaching accident. Harry was only sixteen when he inherited his titles. At that age, he had to become father to his baby brother. And I tried to be a mother to him."

"How very sad," Kate murmured. "But he was fortunate to have you."

"And I've been fortunate to have him. Harry does everything to see to my health and comfort. Why, just yesterday he rode all the way to Cheltenham to see a painting I've been wishing to find. It was painted by my grandfather, and it means a great deal to me."

So it was for his grandmother's sake he came to Rendell Hall to see our painting, she thought. Aloud, she said, "He's been searching for it for a long while, I understand."

"Yes, but he succeeded this time."

"Did he really?"

"Yes, and I'm delighted with it. I've just this morning sent it out to be reframed. I can't wait to hang it over the mantel in our library as soon as we return to Ainsworth Park. You must come one day to see it."

"I should like that very much," Kate said.

Her ladyship took a sip of her tea before returning to her subject. "So you can see why I would naturally think Harry the best of men, but truly, Kate, I'm not alone in my view. It's shared by everyone who knows him."

"Not everyone, I'm afraid," Kate blurted out. As soon as the words left her lips, she regretted them. She stretched her hand across the table. "Forgive me, your ladyship. I shouldn't have—"

"Of course you should." Lady Ainsworth patted the outstretched hand comfortingly. "I want you to be honest with me. You had someone in mind when you made that remark. Who was it who finds such serious fault with my Harry?"

Kate withdrew her hand and rubbed her forehead with it. She was angry with herself for letting this conversation go so far. "I don't wish to malign the man who means so much to you," she said gently.

"Please!" Lady Ainsworth begged.

Kate winced, but surrendered. "I was thinking of a certain Gussie Landers," she mumbled.

Lady Ainsworth's eyebrows drew together in surprise, causing her pince-nez to fall from her nose. "Gussie Landers? I'd heard that the chit had taken ill, but what has my Harry to do with it?"

"I was told," Kate related reluctantly, "that he raised her expectations at a dance and then ignored her in the most humiliating way."

"Good heavens!" her ladyship exclaimed. "Is *that* what's eating the girl? Then this whole *contretemps* must be my fault."

"Your fault? How can that be?"

"Because I made him do it." Her ladyship sat back in her chair, wrinkling her brow in her effort to remember the details. "It was at Almacks, if I recall. I'd forced Harry to accompany me, and, because he didn't wish to be there at all, he was lounging about, sulking. I was quite annoyed with him, I can tell you, and I ordered him to dance with someone. 'Since you're giving me orders,' he grumbled, 'you may as well choose my partner.' So I saw poor Gussie sitting there behind her mother, looking utterly miserable, and I told him to stand up with her. Never saw a face brighten up so quickly as Gussie's did when Harry approached her." She leaned forward anxiously. "I thought we'd done a good turn for the girl."

"But what about afterward?" Kate prodded.

"I never gave it another thought afterward," Lady Ainsworth said bluntly. "And neither did Harry, I'd wager. No reason why we should, is there?"

"I don't know," Kate admitted.

"As I understand the rules, dancing with the same young woman *three* times in one evening does have significance, but only as a sign that the gentleman is interested in her, not a commitment to wedlock. Therefore, it seems clear that standing up with a young woman only once has no significance at all. It certainly doesn't oblige the fellow to woo her. Gussie Landers must be a very foolish girl."

"I suppose you're right," Kate said in a small, shamed voice.

This time it was Lady Ainsworth who stretched her arm across the table. "Open your mind to my Harry, if not your heart," she said, squeezing Kate's hand affectionately. "What you learn might change your life."

Later, walking back to Queen's Square, Kate thought about Lady Ainsworth's words. Perhaps it *was* time for her to open her mind. As for her heart, that was opened long ago.

TWENTY-NINE

❧❧❧

Deirdre was pacing about her bedroom like a caged tiger. Several hours earlier she'd sent a note to Harry's room asking to see him, but now the sun was setting, and there was no sign of him. For the fifth time that afternoon, she sent for Pruitt. "Has he come yet?" she asked.

"No, Miss, not yet," Pruitt said patiently.

"Well, when he does, don't put him in the sitting room if anyone else is in there. If it's occupied, put him in the morning room. Or any room that's unoccupied. And come up for me at once."

"Yes, Miss," the butler said with a barely suppressed sigh of annoyance. "So you've told me, Miss. Several times."

It was dark when the butler knocked at her door again. "A note for you, Miss Deirdre."

"Did Harry—Lord Ainsworth—bring it?"

"No, Miss. A footman delivered it."

"Very well, Pruitt," she said, her eyes on the note. "Thank you."

She closed her door, sat down on her bed, and tore the note open. *Dear Beautiful Deirdre,* it read, *throw on your cloak and come out at once. I have a surprise for you. My carriage awaits you. H. G.*

With a cry of delight, she jumped up, snatched a cloak from the wardrobe, and ran down the stairs.

Pruitt heard her and came to the door. "Are you going out, Miss?" he asked. "Lady Madge has ordered dinner in half an hour."

"Yes, Pruitt, dear Pruitt," she chirped happily, kissing his cheek. "I am indeed going out. And if I'm not back for dinner, tell Mama not to worry."

"You'll need a warmer cloak, Miss," the butler called after her. "It's blowing up something fierce."

But Deirdre paid no mind. Pruitt, shaking his head at the impulsive ways of young women, watched as she ran out the door and down to a carriage that stood waiting just outside the gate. A gentleman (whose wide-brimmed hat was pulled down over his eyes so low that Pruitt couldn't see his face) emerged from the carriage as if to help her in. But Deirdre stopped short and seemed about to turn back. The gentleman, however, put a hand on her arm and, to Pruitt's eyes, seemed almost to shove her inside. The carriage set off at once.

Pruitt stood staring after the disappearing equipage, puzzled. His young mistress had left the house so eagerly, and yet, if his eyes didn't deceive him, she'd been less than eager to climb up into the carriage. She appeared to be pushed into it against her will.

The butler didn't know what to do. He didn't wish to cause an unnecessary scene, but if Miss Deirdre became the victim of some sort of chicanery, he would surely be remiss for not reporting it. Reporting the matter to Lord Quigley, however, would certainly lead to an explosion of temper. His Lordship would surely find fault with him. "What sort of yellow-livered coward are you?" he'd shout. "Couldn't you have stopped the child?"

Perhaps relating the incident to Lady Madge might be the wisest thing to do.

A short while later, Madge tapped on Kate's door. Although Megan explained that Kate was dressing for dinner, Madge brushed past her. "Kate, my love, I think something's amiss. I must speak to you alone."

Megan didn't need to be told to take herself off. As soon as she'd gone, Madge handed Kate a crumpled note. "Pruitt thinks that Deirdre may have been abducted," she said in a choked voice.

"Abducted?" The very word made no sense to Kate. "That's insane!"

"Perhaps it's not so insane. I checked her room and found this note."

Kate scanned it quickly. "H. G.? Who can that be?"

Madge wrung her hands. "Can it be our Harry? He is a Gerard."

Kate shook her head. "This wording doesn't sound like Harry. Nor can I imagine him ever even *thinking* of abducting an innocent girl. I have it on excellent authority, including your own, that he is the most honorable sort."

"Then who can it be?" She wrung her hands in helpless agitation. "It couldn't be Leonard. Certainly not Leonard."

Kate sank down on her bed and studied the missive carefully. "I think I recognize the hand," she said at last. "After all, I've had notes from him all my life."

Madge's eyes widened. "Not . . . not your Percy!"

"Yes, Aunt Madge. As you well know from the scene enacted in your sitting room yesterday, 'my' Percy has been mooning over Deirdre for quite a while."

"Then it may not be an abduction after all," Madge suggested with a glimmer of hope. "It may be an elopement! Do you think they've eloped?"

"No, I don't. If that was their plan, why would he sign Harry's initials? Besides, Deirdre told me she doesn't love Percy after all."

Madge's full bosom heaved, and she sank down on the bed beside her niece. "Then Pruitt is right," she intoned funereally. "She *has* been abducted."

"Let's be certain. Tell Pruitt to come up."

Pruitt entered Kate's bedroom and, not accustomed to seeing his mistress and her guest in their robes, looked down at his shoes uneasily. "You wanted to speak to me?"

"Yes, Pruitt," Kate said. "I understand you think Miss Deirdre was urged into a coach against her will."

"I can't be certain, Miss Kate," the butler said. "She came running downstairs happy as a lark. She'd been eager to see Lord Ainsworth all afternoon, so I thought 'twas him she was meeting. But when she went outside, and the gentleman climbed out of the carriage, she stopped short, like she'd changed her mind. And then, well, it seemed to me he forced her up the steps and into it."

"That gentleman," Kate asked, "was it Lord Ainsworth?"

"I don't think so. He seemed smaller. More like Sir Percy, I'd say."

Madge and Kate exchanged looks. "Thank you, Pruitt, that will be all," Kate said.

"Please, Pruitt," Madge added, "say nothing about this to anyone."

Pruitt bowed himself out. Kate, discouraged by the butler's report, sat down on the bed again. "I think you guessed the truth of it, Aunt Madge. Percy's run off with her. That blasted mawworm never could accept no for an answer."

Madge covered her face with trembling hands. "Now Charles will go riding after them," she moaned, "and there'll be a duel, and I'll be a widow before morning!"

"No, no, it needn't be that way." Kate jumped to her feet. "Look at me, Aunt Madge," she said, lifting her aunt's chin. "Don't tell Uncle Charles just yet. I'll get her back."

Madge eyed her dubiously. "But how?"

Yes, how? Kate asked herself. But it might very well be possible. She knew Percy's stylish carriage was a slug. If she could borrow Leonard's neat little gig and one of his fine horses, she could easily catch up to them. She took her aunt in a comforting embrace. "You keep everything quiet here at home and leave the rest of it to me."

Madge, determined to do her part, did her best to smile through dinner, although her heart was quaking. When Isabel and Charles asked about the two missing young ladies, Madge explained their absence with a shrug. "Probably went off to another concert at the Upper Rooms," she said, hoping no one would notice the tremor in her voice and the trembling of her limbs. "We shall give them a good scold tomorrow for not asking our leave."

Charles and Isabel had no reason not to believe her.

Pruitt, however, was not as successful in keeping the matter secret. Shortly after the remains of the dinner had been removed, the knocker sounded. When he discovered it was Lord Ainsworth at the door, he heaved a sigh of relief. "I'm so happy to see you, Lord Ainsworth," he said with a wide, un-butler-like smile.

Harry, his mind concentrating on his long-anticipated confrontation with Kate, didn't notice the butler's effusive greeting. "May I see her *now?*" he asked determinedly.

The butler's face became serious. "No, my lord," he said. "She's gone."

"Gone? I don't understand. Where has she gone?"

"Wish I could say, my lord. We've no idea where he's taken her."

"He?" Harry peered at the butler in confusion. "Who's he?"

"Sir Percy, my lord. At first they thought it might be you, but I told them it couldn't be. The fellow that abducted her was much smaller than you. And now that you're standing here, it's plain that I was right."

"Good God!" Harry exclaimed, paling. "Are you saying Percy *made off* with her? When?"

"Not more than two hours ago, I'd say."

Harry couldn't quite take it in. "The fool actually abducted her? Unbelievable!" But he had to believe it; the butler couldn't have concocted such a tale. Kate had actually been abducted! He felt a sharp stab of alarm. "Has anyone gone after them?" he asked urgently.

"Not that I know of, my lord."

"Blast! Why the devil not?"

"Don't know, my lord."

Harry's brows knit as he made some quick calculations. "Good thing I brought my curricle," he muttered. "I don't suppose that fool took her away in his phaeton, did he? That high-perch, peacocky thing with the yellow wheels?"

"Why, yes!" Pruitt exclaimed. "Now you mention it, my lord, I remember seeing those very wheels."

"That's one bit of luck, anyway. He can't make any speed in that showy contraption." Harry swung about and made for the door. "I suppose the bumble-brained coxcomb headed north," he muttered as he ran off. "Just wait till I get my hands on him!"

THIRTY

꧁꧂

When Kate was admitted to the Tyndale lodgings, she was shivering from the cold. There was snow in the air, she felt sure of it. Snow would surely complicate her problem. But she could not worry about that possibility now. Her first task was to convince Leonard to lend her the gig.

When Leonard's valet, Hawkins, admitted her to the sitting room, it was plain that she'd interrupted a quarrel between Sir Edward and his son. Hawkins had evidently been packing a trunk, which stood open in the center of the room. Leonard was throwing garments willy-nilly into it, and his father was staring out of the window, tightlipped. The strained silence between them was palpable.

Kate looked from one to the other. "I'm sorry to break in on you like this," she said, "but I have a favor to ask of Leonard."

Sir Edward turned from the window. "Leonard is insisting on going home this very evening," he said, "regardless of my wishes that we remain."

"I told you, sir," Leonard said impatiently, "that you are welcome to remain here without me. You have good reason to stay. I have not."

"If you weren't so hot-headed," his father argued, "you, too, might find a reason. Perhaps Deirdre realizes she made a mistake and wants your forgiveness."

"She'll never have my forgiveness, so please drop the subject. Besides, I'm sure Kate doesn't wish to be a witness to our disagreements."

Kate took this as an opportunity to break in. "Don't trouble yourself about me, Leonard, for I feel like part of your family. I hope you won't mind my saying that your father makes a good point. Deirdre realized she'd made an error very soon after you left, and she tried to break it off with Sir Percy. I'm afraid that, in his anger and disappointment, he's abducted her."

"What?" Leonard ceased his packing. "Abducted her?"

"Yes, more than an hour ago."

Leonard ran a hand through his mane of red hair. "The little fool," he muttered. "Serves her right."

"Leonard!" his father chastised. "That's a dreadful thing to say!"

"Not any more dreadful than what she did to me. I'm sorry, Kate, but if you've come to ask me to rescue her, my answer is no. I will not dance to her tune. Let someone else get her out of this fix."

"Leonard Tyndale," Sir Edward roared, his face reddening as if he were having an attack of apoplexy, "never did I dream I'd raised my son to be a vengeful craven! I'm ashamed of you."

"No, please, Sir Edward," Kate said, taking his hand to calm him. "I didn't come to ask Leonard to go after Deirdre himself. Not under the present circumstances." She turned to Leonard. "I only came to ask if I might borrow your gig."

"Of course, if you need it," Leonard said. "But why?"

"Because it's faster than the great lumbering thing that Charles used to carry us here. If I had a swift, light vehicle like your gig, I could probably catch up with Percy in an hour or two. His phaeton is a slug."

"Are you saying," Sir Edward cried in alarm, "that you mean to follow them yourself?"

"Yes," Kate said calmly. "Why not?"

"Because, my dear, a young woman can't go traipsing over the countryside alone after dark. It can't be done!"

"It *must* be done," Kate said firmly. "I am no missish young girl, you know. I'm a twenty-four-year-old spinster who knows how to take care of herself. So, Leonard, if you please, tell your man to ready your gig for me. I haven't time to spare."

Leonard fixed her with a look of disgust. "Oh, good, ma'am. Very good. A very good ruse indeed. You knew your offer to go after them would tweak my conscience." He gave his trunk a furious kick. "Well, Kate, your ruse worked. You win. I'll go after her myself."

Kate's eyes widened in sincere surprise. "It was no ruse, I swear! I had no intention of tricking you. Please, Leonard, let me be on my way without further ado." But he was already pulling on his greatcoat. "Is Percy driving that high-perch clunker with the yellow wheels?" he asked.

Kate frowned. "If you insist on going," she said in resignation, "then I'm going with you."

"Don't be foolish," Sir Edward objected. "Even a spinster, which you certainly are not, cannot go riding through the night alone with a man."

"Yes, I can, and I will," Kate insisted.

Leonard shrugged. "Don't argue with her, sir. Kate is not a female who easily changes her mind. I'll take Hawkins along to observe the proprieties. Come, Kate, let's be on our way."

THIRTY-ONE

❧❧❧

Harry tried to keep his fury in check as he drove his curricle over the dark road. Once the brightness of Bath was left behind, his only source of light was the dim glow from a pair of lanterns mounted on the sides of the cab. This dimness kept him from indulging in the excessive speed he would have liked. To make matters worse, an early spring storm seemed to be brewing. A bitterly cold wind was blowing right into his face, and it smelled of snow. Fortunately, he'd worn a wool scarf. He wound it tighter about his neck.

He wished he could move faster. He wanted, more than he'd ever wanted anything, to pull Kate from the arms of her abductor and into his own. He hadn't realized before the extent to which he'd become attached to her. He'd felt an attraction the very first time he'd laid eyes on her—or perhaps even earlier, when he'd seen the painting of the girl she so very closely resembled. He'd found it as hard, that day, to tear his eyes from the painting as from the girl herself.

That attraction had grown with each successive meeting, despite the impediments she kept throwing in his path. In Bath, he'd been utterly delighted to come upon her. Her apparent resistance to his attentions didn't trouble him, for when he understood the reason, he was more entertained than frustrated, for he was sure she cared for him, too. He had every confidence that he was about to break through that resistance very soon. Even his grandmother, whose feminine instincts regarding the mysteries of human behavior were remarkably keen, had hinted that his pursuit of the girl would be successful. He'd been—he had to admit it!—quite complacent. Tonight, however, he found himself shaken out of that complacency. Percy's despicable act had inflicted upon him so great an agony of concern for Kate's safety that it was a physical pain in his chest. That pain awoke in him an awesome awareness of the depth of his feelings toward her. *In the game of love*, he thought ruefully, *the heart wears no protection against pain.*

The thought of what Kate might be feeling now as Percy's prisoner only increased his agony. He warned himself that he must not think of the nauseating possibilities—of her terror, increasing as the hours passed . . . of her helplessness . . . of Percy's hands touching her. He must concentrate only on his course of action. That blasted clunch was probably taking her to Gretna Green to force her into a quick Scottish wedding. Because even at top speed it would take Percy two days to reach Gretna, Kate would have to spend at least one night alone with her abductor. To save her reputation, she'd be forced to agree to the marriage. That situation was what Harry had to prevent.

They were three hours ahead of him, he reasoned, but he, with his well-sprung curricle and two lively horses, could cover the same distance in half the time. They would have to find an inn sometime before midnight. He would ride for an hour and then begin to check every inn he passed. If the snow held off, he could, with any luck, discover them before any real damage was done.

He'd driven less than an hour when he passed the first inn. The wooden sign whose hinges creaked in the bitter wind read The Red Falcon. He decided not to investigate, for it was unlikely that Percy would stop so soon. He was just hurtling past when his eye caught a glimpse of something yellow in front of the inn's stable yard. He slowed down his horses, abruptly wheeled the curricle around, and drove it into the inn's gravel driveway. One look was enough to prove to him it was indeed Percy's phaeton. A second look explained why Percy had stopped so soon. The phaeton had a broken wheel. Harry sighed in relief—he'd found his quarry!

He gave over his horses to the care of an ostler, ran across the innyard, entered the taproom, and looked about him. A few patrons were still drinking their ale at this late hour. The innkeeper, filling a mug from a spigotted barrel, did not bother to look round to discover who'd just come in. "You, there," Harry called to him, "I'm looking for a fellow who came in perhaps an hour ago."

"Dandified chap?" the innkeeper asked, glancing at Harry over his shoulder. "With a lady?"

"That's right. Where——?"

"Took the private parlor," the innkeeper said, concentrating on his pouring. "Door over there, to yer left."

Harry strode across the room and kicked open the door. A quick glance revealed a small parlor with a table at the center. At the far side of the table sat a startled Percy, his feet resting on an empty chair at his side and a glass in his hand. He gaped at the intruder, frozen.

Harry closed the door behind him. "Where is she?" he asked threateningly.

"Harry!" Percy croaked. "How——?"

"Where *is* she?" His voice was quieter but more dangerous.

Percy's feet came down, and he inched his chair back slowly. "How d-did you find me?" he asked nervously.

Harry walked round the table and grasped Percy's neckcloth in one powerful fist. "I asked you a question," he said between clenched teeth. Pulling the neckcloth tight, he used it to lift Percy to his feet. "Tell me!"

"What right have you to ask?" Percy said in frightened self-defense. "We're eloping."

"Balderdash!" Harry sneered. "As if she'd run off with a mawworm like you. She'd sooner wed your valet." He gave the neckcloth one more twist. "I'll ask for the last time. Where is she?"

"Th-There," Percy choked out, pointing to a door to his right. " 'S a b-bedroom. She's sleeping."

"Sleeping?" Harry, in surprised disbelief, eased his hold. "She'd never—"

Percy caught his breath before he began his explanation. "She was screaming and carrying on so loudly I had to do something." He dropped his eyes guiltily. "I put a drop of laudanum in her tea."

"You damnable make-bait, you drugged her!" Harry said in disgust, "I ought to choke the life out of you!" He slammed the shivering fellow against the wall, dropped his hold, and ran across the room to the bedroom door.

"You won't be able to wake her," Percy said. "She'll be out for hours yet."

Harry threw the door open. Except for a small glow from a tiny fireplace, the room was dark. On the bed he could barely make out the shadowed figure huddled under a pile of bedclothes. But he could hear her stertorous breathing. The only other sounds were the crackle of the burning logs and a tapping at the room's little window. *Damnation*, Harry thought, *it's sleeting.*

He backed out of the room and softly closed the door. There was no point in waking her now. Even without the problem of the sleet, it would be almost impossible to get her back to Bath before four or five. It would be wiser to wait for daylight.

He stalked back to where Percy stood cowering against the wall. "You miserable cur," he said, grasping his neckcloth again. "If I discover that you so much as laid a hand on her, I'll run you through with that fire iron!"

"Of course I didn't!" Percy insisted, offended. "What do you take me for? I was going to marry her!"

"Yes, marry her whether she wanted to or not. You planned all this, didn't you? A scheme to keep her out all night so that she'd *have* to marry you! I ought to run you through anyway. But I think that giving you a sound thrashing with my fives may be a sufficient lesson."

As he raised a fist, poor Percy lifted a shaking hand to protect his swollen chin. "Not my jaw," he cried. "Not again."

He made such a pathetic picture that Harry's anger died. He released his hold, and Percy slipped to the floor. Harry turned away, threw himself down on the nearest chair, and unwound the scarf from about his neck. "I hope it won't sleet all night," he remarked.

Percy picked himself up. "You've ruined my neck-cloth," he whined.

"Consider yourself lucky that it's all I've ruined," Harry retorted.

Percy cautiously made his way to the table. Getting no reaction from his adversary, he sat down. "But do you consider *yourself* lucky?" he asked. "There are consequences for you in this matter as well as for me. Her family will expect *you* to marry her, now, you know. After all, you won't be able to get her home before morning."

"I suppose that's true," Harry said, mulling over Percy's words. A slow smile brightened his face.

"Well, I don't mind. That was my eventual intention in any case."

Percy gawked at him. "You intended to marry her? All along?"

"Ever since I first laid eyes on her. Why are you so surprised?"

"But I thought . . . are you saying you had designs on her even though Leonard's your best friend?"

"What has Leonard to say to it?" Harry asked.

"Nothing, I suppose," Percy shrugged, "now that she's broken it off with him."

"Broken *what* off with him?" Harry inquired, a fearful suspicion beginning to take root inside him that they were not speaking of the same person.

"Of course," Percy mused, "I assumed she'd make it up with him after she threw me over. I had no idea that you and she . . ."

Though Harry's mind did not yet grasp what Percy was saying, his innards did. They knew he'd made a terrible mistake. His stomach turned over, and his heart did a flip-flop in his chest. "Hold on there, Percy," he said with a gulp. "It can't be Kate you're babbling about."

"Kate?" Percy gaped at him. "Why would I be speaking of Kate?"

Harry put up a hand, as if to stop a runaway horse. "Then, confound it, man, who is it sleeping in that room?"

The bedroom door opened at that moment, and a disheveled, tear-stained figure stumbled into the parlor. The expression on her face showed sheer terror, but at her first glimpse of the new arrival, it took on a glow like a morning sky. "Harry!" she cried joyfully. "You've come to rescue me! I knew you would!"

"Good God!" Harry gasped, wincing. "It's *Deir-dre!*"

THIRTY-TWO

⋰⋰⋰

Leonard chose to take his phaeton rather than his lighter gig, first because it could provide some protection against the rising winds, and second because it accommodated two horses rather than the one-horsed gig. Even with a heavier vehicle like the phaeton, two horses were better than one.

As he and Kate waited for the horses to be readied, they discussed some of the possible routes the abductor might have taken. There were really only two likely routes—east to London or north to Gretna. "It's Gretna, certainly," Kate insisted.

"I don't see why you're so sure," Leonard said dubiously.

"Because," Kate answered promptly, "Percy's not the sort to take a girl to London to use for his pleasure. His object is wedlock, not debauchery."

Convinced, Leonard set out toward the north.

Riding into the wind that was roaring down from the north, they could not make good time. It was more than an hour before they trotted past The Red Falcon Inn. Reasoning that Percy must have gone farther before stopping, they went on. Two hours later, having made two fruitless stops at roadside inns, and with the sleet icing the road dangerously, Leonard held a whispered conversation with his man Hawkins. Then he turned to Kate. "We can't go any farther," he said in despair. "I suspect Percy will try to reach Worcester before stopping for the night, and we're not even halfway there. I've slid off the road twice already. The blasted sleet makes it hard for me to see. I'm afraid we must turn back at once, or we may not get back home tonight at all."

Kate could not disagree. In miserable silence they started back. Leonard peered out into the darkness, trying to make out the edges of the road. Hawkins hung out the window on the right, trying to keep the sleet from accumulating on the glass of the lantern, while Kate tried to do the same on her side. None of them had the heart to say a word.

It was well toward morning when Kate spotted The Red Falcon Inn again. "Please, Leonard," she pleaded, "let's stop here for a while, just to get warm. I can't even feel my fingers anymore."

He did as she asked. They entered the taproom, hoping to find someone to serve them a hot drink, but the place was deserted. Even the fire in the huge fireplace was banked. "I'll find the kitchen," Hawkins said, making his way toward a door at the rear, "an' get us somethin' 'ot to drink."

Kate noticed a dim light coming from a doorway to their left. Hoping to find a fire, she went to the door and threw it open. What she saw made her gasp so loudly that Leonard came running up behind her. There was Harry, right in front of them, seated at a table with Deirdre kneeling before him, her head resting in his lap. And Percy, the cause of all this turmoil, standing near the fire fussing with his neckcloth.

At the sound of the opening door, all three looked up. Deirdre gave a glad cry. "Kate! How wonderful!"

Leonard, in relief at seeing her safe, reacted as a mother might when her lost child is restored to her. Instead of embracing the child, a mother sometimes shakes him in fury, with words like: "You naughty creature, how could you frighten your mother that way!" Leonard experienced the same fury. "*Wonderful?*" he snarled. "We've ridden all night through the most punishing winds and sleet in search of you, only to find you calmly sitting there with your head on Harry's lap, and *wonderful* is all you have to say?"

"But you needn't have gone to all that trouble," Deirdre said with a trilling laugh. "Harry came after me, and he saved me, and he's going to marry me, so everything's absolutely wonderful!"

"Marry you!" Kate asked, aghast.

Harry's eyes met hers. They seemed to be pleading for her to understand, but Kate did not understand at all. What had happened here?

"So Harry's going to marry you, is he?" Leonard

snapped. "Wonderful, indeed!" He stormed into the room. "I'll show you something wonderful. First, you, Harry Gerard, for betraying our friendship and stealing my betrothed behind my back!" With that he struck Harry a smart blow to the eye. Harry's chair toppled over, sending him to the floor with a loud crash.

Deirdre screamed and ran to Harry's side.

But Leonard paid no heed. He swung round to Percy. "And you, Greenway, for abducting the girl. Take this!" Before Percy could protect himself, he was struck on the jaw again and fell to the floor.

Hawkins appeared in the doorway at that moment, bearing a heavily loaded tray. Ignoring the chaos like a proper gentleman's gentleman, he asked, "Does anyone wish a cup o' 'ot tea?"

"Never mind the tea," Leonard said, motioning him to set down the tray. "I think we've warmed up enough."

Kate, meanwhile, stood rooted to her spot in the doorway, too benumbed by shock to move. Deirdre's news had struck her a terrible blow—a wound that numbs before the pain sets in. She did not yet feel the pain, but she knew she soon would. It came as a great surprise to her—greater than the news of the betrothal itself—that the wound was so severe. She'd been aware that she was attracted to Harry, but she hadn't realized the extent of it. *How could I have been so foolish,* she asked herself, *as to have let myself fall in love so deeply?*

Leonard, after surveying the chaos he'd caused,

turned to her. "Let's go home, Kate. There's nothing more for us here."

"Wait a moment, Leonard," Harry said, lifting himself on one elbow. "Whether or not you realize it, you are needed. Did you come in your phaeton?"

"Yes," answered Leonard tightly. "Why?"

"You see, Percy's carriage has a broken wheel, and I came in my curricle, which would not be a satisfactory equipage in this weather. So, awkward as it is to ask it of you under the circumstances, I'd be obliged if you took Deirdre home with you."

Leonard sighed. "I suppose I must. Very well. Deirdre, go and get your cloak."

Deirdre got up, and with a last, loving look at Harry, went to the bedroom.

Leonard looked down at the unconscious Percy. "I suppose you'd like me to take him back, too," he muttered.

Harry got up, and both men stood looking down at the prone figure sprawled on the floor. "It would be a favor to me if you would," Harry said.

"Then help me lift him up. Hawkins, give us a hand here."

They set Percy erect, and, with Hawkins holding him up under one arm and Leonard the other, they dragged Percy's limp body to the door. "I'll wait in the carriage for you, Kate," Leonard said, and they carried their burden out.

Kate was about to follow him, but she took one last look at Harry. This man, whom she'd so often thought of as a rake, looked anything but rakish now. His dark hair was dishevelled, the skin under his eye was already turning purple, his clothes were rumpled, and, worst of all, the look on his face was one of abject misery. As she watched, he sank down at the table and dropped his head in his hands. If he was at all elated by his betrothal, he gave no sign of it.

As if she were guided by some outside force, Kate went up to him and put a hand on his shoulder. "It was noble of you to have done this," she said softly. "You saved Deirdre from terrible disgrace."

"Noble?" He gave a mirthless laugh. "It was idiotic!"

"Idiotic? I don't understand."

"Don't you see?" His voice shook with self-mockery. "I thought I was saving *you*."

THIRTY-THREE

❧❦❧

Madge managed to keep her secret all evening long, although her agony increased as the hours passed. When Charles and Isabel complained about their daughters' keeping such late hours, Madge made excuses for them. This did not assuage Charles. "One would think they'd hurry home on so cold an evening," he muttered. "I, for one, will make an early night of it and get under the covers. But when I hear those young ladies come in, I intend to get up and give them a good scolding."

The women agreed on an early evening, and they all went to bed. In spite of swearing he'd wait up for his daughter and his niece, Charles fell promptly asleep. Madge, however, could not. The tall clock in the master bedroom struck two, and then three, but there was no sign of Deirdre's or Kate's return. Madge's terror for the safety of her daughter—and her niece, too—grew with every passing minute.

She lit a candle to watch the clock, but hours pass incredibly slowly when one watches the minute hand inch its way round the clock's face. By four, Madge found the wait unbearable. She rose from her bed and, taking her still-burning candle, stole out of her bedroom. She made her way down the corridor to Isabel's room and tapped at the door. It took a long while before Isabel peeped out. One glance at Madge's face was enough to frighten her. "Madge?" she asked tensely. "What's amiss?"

"I'm sorry I woke you," Madge whispered, "but I'm out of my mind with worry."

"I wasn't sleeping." Isabel drew her in and closed the door. "I'm worried, too. The girls aren't home. Where can they be at this hour?"

"I can tell you that . . . in part, at least. I should have told you before. Percy had abducted Deirdre, and Kate went after them."

It took several minutes for Isabel to get a full explanation. By the time she understood all the circumstances, she was quite pale, and Madge was abrim with tears. "I shall have to tell Charles," she wept, "and he'll go to find them, and who knows what will happen then. And Deirdre will have been out all night with that bounder, and if she's not to be considered damaged goods on the marriage mart, she'll have to wed him!"

"You once thought Percy was good enough for my Kate," Isabel pointed out with asperity.

"Yes, but that was before I knew what a cad he was."

"He's not really a cad," Isabel said, trying to be fair. "Merely impulsive."

"Huh!" Madge sneered. "I would not call abducting an innocent young girl an impulse. I'd call it a heinous crime!"

The words had scarcely left her lips when they heard a noise down below. They ran out to the corridor to discover Kate leading a wilting Deirdre up the stairs. "Oh, heavens," Madge cried, swooping down on them, "what has happened to my darling child?"

Deirdre lifted her head and favored her mother with a glowing smile. "It's wonderful, Mama! Everything's wonderful."

"She's only sleepy," Kate explained. "Percy gave her a dose of laudanum. She'll be fine by tonight."

Madge took her daughter in her arms. "Come, my love, come. I'll put you to bed. You can tell us everything when you wake."

Charles, awakened by the commotion, came waddling out of the bedroom. "What's going on?" he asked loudly, the ball at the tail of his nightcap bouncing against his nose, "What kept you out till this ungodly hour?"

"Harry saved me," Deirdre said, beaming sleepily at everyone. "Saved me in the nick of time. We're betrothed. And everything's wonderful."

"Go back to bed, Charles," Madge said. "I'll explain later. Let me get this poor child to bed."

He opened his mouth to object, but a warning signal

from Isabel made him restrain himself. With a grunt, he turned on his heel and returned to the bedroom.

"If you'll excuse me," Kate said wanly, "I'll go to bed, too."

Isabel, with brows knit, watched her daughter walk away. Her motherly instincts told her that something was very wrong, but with both girls evidently safe and sound, she could not fathom what it was. As soon as she helped Madge get Deirdre into bed, she ran off to Kate's room.

Kate's bedroom was dark. The morning light, just beginning to filter in through the gaps in the draperies, did not yet give enough light for Isabel to see her daughter clearly. She could barely make out Kate's form, an unmoving shadow seated on the edge of the bed. Isabel came in and sat down beside her. Now, up close, she could see that Kate had made no attempt to undress. The girl was just sitting there staring at nothing. "What is it, my love?" she asked gently.

Kate blinked and tried to clear her head. "Everything's wonderful, didn't you hear Deirdre say so?" she asked in a weary voice.

"But you don't find it so?" Isabel asked.

"No, I don't."

Isabel put an arm about the girl's shoulders. "Can you not tell me what happened?"

"There's not much to tell. When Leonard and I found the inn where Percy had taken her, Harry had already discovered them. With an offer of marriage, he rescued dear little Deirdre from—what is it they call it in Mrs. Radcliffe's romances?—a fate worse than death."

The bitter irony in Kate's voice proved to Isabel what she'd already suspected—that Kate had fallen in love with Harry Gerard. In the still-dim light, she peered at her daughter's face—the pale cheeks, the clouded eyes, the tense little muscle that twitched just above her jaw. As mothers everywhere and forever are wont to do, she wished she could suffer her daughter's pain in her stead. But no one can take on another's pain. Sore at heart, she lifted her hand and smoothed back a strand of Kate's hair. "My poor darling," she murmured sadly, "does Harry's commitment to Deirdre hurt you so?"

Kate had held herself together through the long ride home, but her mother's sympathy caused her self-possession to crumble. With a low cry, she threw herself into her mother's arms. "Oh, Mama, how can I bear it?" she wept.

Isabel rocked the sobbing girl in her arms, her own tears flowing freely down her cheeks. When at last the sobs subsided, Isabel pulled out a large handkerchief from her bosom and wiped both their cheeks. "Perhaps we should cut this visit short," she suggested.

Kate lifted her head and twisted her tear-swollen lips into a sad smile. "Yes, please, Mama," she said gratefully. "Let's go home!"

THIRTY-FOUR

❦

When she was sure that Kate had at last fallen
asleep, Isabel went down to the sitting room, sat down
at the writing table, and wrote a note to Sir Edward.
It was, she had to admit, abruptly worded: *Please meet
me at ten this morning at the corner where Brooke
Street meets the Circus. I. R.* But she was in no mood
for embellishments. She sent it off just as it was.

She was standing on the Brooke Street corner right
on time. Although the winter weather of the night before had eased considerably and the sleet that had iced
the streets was rapidly melting, it was quite chilly. She
hoped Edward would not keep her waiting, but at that
very moment she saw him approaching. Although her
present mood was not a happy one, the sight of him
made her smile. "You're wearing trousers!" she exclaimed as soon as he'd made his bow.

"A small price to pay to win your forgiveness, ma'am," he said, taking her arm.

"Oh, bosh," she said scornfully as they proceeded to stroll round the Circus, "I've told you I have nothing to forgive. You called me fat, but it was nothing but the truth."

He stopped in his tracks and dropped her arm. "I did not call you fat!" he declared, reddening angrily. "I never said such a thing, and I don't want ever again to hear you accuse me of it."

"My word, Edward, you needn't have an attack of apoplexy over it," Isabel said in amusement.

"I'll have apoplexy if I wish! The truth is, ma'am, I find you to be quite the most beautiful woman of my acquaintance. There! I've said it! Let that be an end of it."

"And very well said, too, my dear," Isabel replied, "but you needn't shout it to the world."

"Sorry," Edward said meekly, his high color receding.

Isabel took back his arm and tucked it under hers, and they proceeded down the street. "I'm glad you said those lovely words, Edward," she admitted, "although I know quite well they were nothing but butter sauce."

"They weren't butter sauce. It's how I see you." He threw her a quick, shy glance. "How a man sees a woman . . . there's a great deal of significance in that, you know."

"Yes, I know." She patted his arm. "But we mustn't

go into that right now. I have something to tell you that you may not like."

"Oh?" He stopped walking and faced her bravely. "Well, spit it out."

"I'm leaving Bath. Kate wants to go home."

"When?"

"Today. This afternoon."

"You couldn't, I suppose, let her go without you."

"No. She needs me, I think."

"Blast!" he swore. "Just when things are going so well with us."

"Yes."

They resumed their stroll, but at a slower pace. "Of course, in a way, your news makes a similar decision easier for me," he admitted. "Leonard is packing at this moment. He's not at all happy. I've told him I intended to stay, but perhaps I should go home with him."

"Yes, you should." She sighed sadly, aware that she was feeling far from serene. "Being a parent requires sacrifices."

"Great sacrifices," he agreed glumly.

By this time, they'd completed the circle and arrived at their starting point. Isabel turned to him and offered her hand. "Then I suppose this is good-bye."

"It needn't be. Certainly not forever." He lifted her hand to his lips. "I shall see you again."

"I hope so."

"You may count on it," he declared firmly. "And in the meantime, if I should send you another gift, you'd better not send it back as you did before."

She smiled. "I won't. I promise."

Having nothing left to say, they made their bows and started off in different directions. After going just a couple of steps, however, Sir Edward suddenly stopped. "And if I should pay a visit," he called after her, "do you promise not to shut the door in my face?"

"I promise," she replied, grinning, "but only if you're wearing those lovely trousers."

When she returned to Queen's Square, Isabel discovered that Charles and Madge were entertaining an early visitor. "Come in to the drawing room," Madge greeted her, "and say hello to Lady Ainsworth. She just dropped by to express her congratulations on Deirdre and Harry's betrothal."

Isabel made her bow and mumbled her good wishes.

"It is good to see you again, Lady Rendell," the elderly woman said, rising from her chair with the help of her cane. "Unfortunately, I must take my leave. Lady Rendell, I wonder, since you're still dressed for the outdoors, if you'd be good enough to see me to my carriage."

"It shall be my pleasure," Isabel said, but she and Madge exchanged questioning glances. It was an unusual request. Isabel wondered, as she offered her arm, if the lady had a purpose in mind.

Lady Ainsworth did not say a word until the outer door closed behind them. Then she looked about to make sure they could not be overheard. "Lady Rendell, what I'm about to say is for your ears alone. May I count on your discretion?"

"Of course," Isabel said, surprised.

"It concerns your daughter. I am very fond of her." She threw Isabel a sharp glance. "And so is my grandson."

"Yes?" Isabel said, carefully noncommittal.

"If Harry weds Deirdre, it will be disastrous for all concerned. I know this, and I suspect you know it, too."

Isabel shook her head. "Even if I agreed with you, your ladyship, I see no help for it."

"There may be help for it. The nuptials are still in the future. And one should never be sure of the future until it is past. One never knows what tricks fate may play."

Isabel eyed her suspiciously. "Your ladyship, are you suggesting that you have some scheme—?"

"Hush!" Lady Ainsworth put a finger to her lips, but her eyes twinkled. "I will only say that, one day soon, you and Kate will receive an invitation to Ainsworth Park. Kate will probably wish to refuse it. I want you to promise me that she will be there."

Isabel felt a ray of hope for the first time since Kate had wept in her arms. "My lady," she said, unable to resist giving the old woman a hug, "whatever your plans are, and whether or not you are successful, you have my everlasting gratitude."

"I don't want your gratitude," Lady Ainsworth retorted, trying to hide her pleasure in Isabel's display of warmth. "I want your promise that Kate will come with you."

Isabel planted a kiss on her cheek. "We'll be there if I have to drag her in chains."

While this exchange was taking place, Harry was knocking at the door of Sir Edward's lodgings. Hawkins opened the door but blocked Harry's way. "Sir Leonard is not seeing visitors today," he said.

"He'll see me," Harry said between clenched teeth, and he pushed Hawkins aside.

He found Leonard sitting on a large settee, dressed for travel except for his boots, one of which he was about to pull on. He looked up at Harry's entrance. "What the devil do *you* want?" he growled.

"What do you think?" Harry retorted. "To return the facer you so generously gave me."

Leonard eyed Harry's swollen eye and the heavily purpled cheek under it with a satisfied smirk. "It's a beauty, I must say."

"Then stand up, you make-bait, and let me return the compliment."

"Why should I?" Leonard pulled on the boot and picked up the other. "It wasn't I who played *you* false."

"If you think I played you false, Leonard Tyndale, you're a greater gudgeon than you look!" Harry snapped. "I never entertained the slightest desire for your Deirdre, and you know it. And if I did, have I ever given you reason to suspect I'd pursue a girl you loved behind your back?"

"Perhaps not," Leonard granted, "but then, why did

you go after her when Percy absconded with her. Why didn't you come to me?"

"Because I didn't go after Deirdre."

"What?" Leonard glared at him. "What sort of twaddle is this?"

Harry slumped down beside him on the settee. "I made a mistake," he said sheepishly. "I thought it was Kate."

Leonard couldn't understand. "Are you saying you thought Percy'd made off with Kate?"

"Yes. You see, I'd gone to call on Kate, and when the butler said she'd been abducted, I stupidly assumed—"

"Why would you assume that Percy would choose Kate? You knew he was wild for Deirdre, didn't you?"

"Yes, but he'd pursued Kate for years before that. All right, dash it all, I admit I was an ass."

Leonard groaned as the full significance of last night's fiasco slowly dawned on him. "Good God, Harry," he exclaimed, "are you saying you're in love with Kate?"

"I'm trying not to say it," Harry said drily. "After all, I'm a gentleman, am I not? A gentleman doesn't admit to loving one girl when he's betrothed to another."

"What a deuced muddle," Leonard muttered.

"Yes, it is," Harry agreed.

They sat side-by-side in silence for a long while. Then Leonard said, "I'm sorry about the facer."

"I'll forgive you, old fellow," Harry said, putting out his hand, "if you'll say we're still friends."

Leonard shook it heartily. "I never thought we weren't."

"You don't say!" Harry fingered his bruised eye. "I never would have guessed."

They laughed, both relieved that last night's unpleasantness seemed to have been overcome. But Harry remained troubled. *Friends!* he thought ruefully. *How can we remain friends when I'm to be wed to the woman he loves?* That was the question they should be facing.

Harry knew he was fully to blame for the muddle they were now in—he'd jumped to a mistaken conclusion about the identity of the girl who'd been abducted, and that mistake had led to everything that followed. Those events had had a terrible inevitability about them. He'd been helplessly tangled in circumstances out of his control. He hadn't realized what a pawn he'd been in the hands of fate until Deirdre had come into the parlor of The Red Falcon Inn and thrown herself into his arms. He could still hear her cries ringing in his ears: *Oh, Harry, my dearest love, you do love me, you do!* How else could he have responded but to offer for her? And now, how could he maintain this friendship when he was taking for his bride the girl his friend so dearly desired?

He knew they should speak to each other openly about this. But perhaps this was not the time. For now, it was enough that they'd shaken hands. The rest could wait.

He picked up his greatcoat and started for the door.

"Well, Leonard, I'm off. I've another score to settle this morning."

"That's strange," Leonard said, pulling on his boot. "So have I."

Harry stopped and wheeled about, at the same moment that Leonard jumped to his feet. Their eyes met, and they both grinned. "*Percy!*" they cried together, and, arm in arm, they strode out the door.

The prospect of "settling the score" with Percy was so satisfying that the vexatious problem they'd avoided discussing was pushed out of their minds. They were positively cheerful when they arrived at Percy's rooms. "Toss a coin to see who gives him the first blow," Leonard suggested.

"Heads," Harry said, tossing.

It was tails. Leonard chortled happily as they banged on the door.

But their good spirits were not to last. Percy, bag and baggage, was gone.

The two friends stood together on the street, chilled by the wind and the disappointment of not having been able to work out their frustrations with their fists. "Well, I've lost my bride, and I've lost my revenge," Leonard muttered, "but at least I still have my best friend."

Harry put up his collar against the wind. It was time, he thought, to face their problem openly. "Can I be your best friend while being wed to Deirdre?" he asked bluntly. "Tell me honestly, Leonard, do you still love her?"

Leonard kicked at a piece of ice still clinging to the

pavement. "I admit, to my everlasting shame, that I do. And probably always will."

"It's strange, because—forgive me, old man—you know as well as I that she's as fickle as a bee in a flower garden. Last week she loved you. Yesterday, it was Percy. Today she loves me. How can you care so greatly for such a maggoty chit?"

"She's still a bit of a child, don't you see?" Leonard said, earnestly trying to defend what in his heart he believed was indefensible. "Perhaps she has to flit about in that flower garden for a while before settling down."

"But she *is* settling down," Harry muttered. "With me."

"Yes," was the glum reply. "I know."

There was nothing more to be said. They shook hands for an unspoken good-bye. "Well, don't look so down, old fellow," Harry said as he started off down the street. "With any luck, she'll discover another flower in the garden and jilt me."

THIRTY-FIVE

❦

I thought I was saving you! Those words echoed over and over in Kate's head for days after returning home. At first they gave her comfort. She took them to mean Harry loved her. The look on his face and the crack in his voice when he'd said them made it plain. He might never be able to declare himself, but he loved her. She used that fact as a secret little talisman that she could carry inside her, to warm her through the lonely nights.

I thought I was saving you! It meant he loved *her,* not Deirdre. It was only the dreadful circumstances of that evening—the fact that Deirdre had spent the night in the inn and could not be permitted to return the next morning with her good name soiled—that had forced him to offer for her. He could not have guessed that Leonard would arrive on the scene. If only she and Leonard had stopped at The Red Falcon earlier, her whole life might have been different.

But as the days passed, this comforting conviction began to fade. *I thought I was saving you.* The words were not necessarily a declaration of love. They could be merely an explanation for how he'd happened to be there. Even though he had come after her, not Deirdre, it could merely have been the act of a gentleman. He might be the sort to rescue any young woman who'd been abducted.

I thought I was saving you. What made her think those words had any significance beyond their literal meaning? After all, he was very quick to get himself betrothed. If he didn't love Deirdre, couldn't he have found a way to avoid offering for her? Couldn't he have taken Leonard aside and urged him to take his place?

The most logical probability, she decided, was that he did love Deirdre. Perhaps he'd loved her all along, but he'd kept his feelings in check because Leonard was his friend. When he discovered he'd rescued her from Percy's clutches, he undoubtedly jumped at the opportunity to claim her for himself. So the words *I thought I was saving you* no longer held the same resonance they'd had at first.

Bereft even of that small consolation, Kate knew there was nothing further to hope for regarding Harry Gerard. He was spoken for, and she had to put him out of her thoughts. She found, to her dismay, that it was very hard to do. Little scenes of the moments they spent together constantly replayed themselves in her mind. The memories, some delicious and some painful, made the days long and the nights endless. She felt listless and depressed. This was not like her. She had to take herself in hand.

What was required, she knew, was self-discipline. She forced herself to follow her usual pursuits: riding her mare like the wind over the back fields, walking briskly to the village on little errands, visiting acquaintances in the neighborhood, dealing with the household staff and the accounts. She did all these things with determination but no pleasure. The result was that she presented a face to the world that was curt and impatient. Everyone noticed the change in her, even her mother.

But Isabel did nothing until the day she overheard one of the gardeners remarking to the stableboy that Miss Kate was turning into a sour old maid.

Isabel could not ignore that. "Do you know, my dear girl," she remarked that evening when they both were together in the sitting room, Isabel with her embroidery and Kate with a book, "that you have not a jot of romance in you?"

Kate did not look up from the page. "I haven't?" she asked absently.

"No, you haven't. Any young woman who's been crossed in love would wander about the house trailing a fluttery silk scarf behind her, moping and sighing and wiping away her tears. You, on the other hand, frown and stride about and snap people's heads off."

Kate merely turned a page. "One copes with one's problems in keeping with one's character," she said. "My character is not romantic, I suppose."

"I know you're suffering, my love," Isabel admitted, "but this hard veneer you've put on to protect yourself seems a bit too thick."

This caused Kate to look up. "It's easy for you to say. You've had a missive from Edward almost every day and—" She pointed to an elegant, inlaid ebony music box placed at the center of the mantlepiece, open at this very moment and emitting a tinkling Haydn melody. "—and that gift box as well."

"But how can I enjoy my letters and gifts when my daughter's turning into a sour old maid before my eyes?"

Kate gulped. "A sour old maid?"

"That's how you're beginning to appear to everyone." It was a hard truth to point out to a beloved daughter. Isabel stitched away at her needlework for a few moments in order to restore her serenity. When she felt she'd regained it, she went on. "I don't know why you're taking Harry's betrothal so badly. After all, you should take some consolation in knowing the fellow loves you."

"I know no such thing," Kate said, and tried to resume her reading.

"Of course you do," Isabel insisted. "Harry told you so himself."

"No, he did not. Just because he thought he was rescuing me, it does not follow that he cared for me."

"He cares for you. I have it on very good authority."

Kate threw aside her book. "Have you indeed? Whose, may I ask?"

"His grandmother's."

"Hmph!" Kate snorted. "What a source! Lady Ainsworth is a dear old soul, and I know she's fond of me. I suspect she'd wish for Harry to care for me the way she does. But you should know better than to take seriously the fanciful ravings of a doddering old woman."

"She's not doddering," Isabel argued angrily. "And they were not fanciful ravings. Why, I'd wager she knows Harry better than anyone else does."

"Rubbish! What independent, self-confident young man would share his deepest feelings with his grandmother? Use your common sense, Mama, and try not to indulge in foolish fancies."

Having delivered that old-maidish scold, Kate picked up her book and buried herself in it. Isabel, however, was too shaken to resume her needlework. *Was Kate right?* she asked herself. She'd placed all her hopes for Kate's future happiness in the words Lady Ainsworth had spoken that day on the street in Bath. There was to be a message. An invitation or some such thing. Here it was, more than a fortnight later, and she'd had no word from Ainsworth Park. Was it possible that those hopes were based on the 'fanciful ravings of a doddering old woman'?

THIRTY-SIX

On the evening after the abduction, Harry presented himself to Charles and formally asked for Deirdre's hand. Charles gave his grateful approval. Madge, fluttery with excitement, suggested that they all sit down together for a celebratory dinner. "Isabel and Kate have gone home to Norfolk, the Tyndales are gone, and my friend, Mrs. Compton, has returned to London, so I've no guests to invite, but if you could coax Lady Ainsworth to join us—"

"My grandmother finds late-evening dinners a bit too much for her, I'm afraid," Harry said apologetically.

Madge forced a smile. "Then there will be only four of us at table, but I'm certain we can make a celebration anyway."

Through the first three courses, it did not seem much like a celebration. Harry's manner was impeccably polite, but he seemed to Madge to be too restrained. Deirdre, although very happy at the turn of events, was still feeling the effects of the laudanum and kept yawning. Charles, who was somewhat in awe of Harry, did not prattle on in his usual manner. And Madge, who suspected that Harry might have been forced by circumstances into this betrothal, was almost miserable. She tried her best, but the dinner conversation was far from sparkling. "This is not much of a celebration for such an auspicious occasion," she admitted ruefully after the Apricot Russe had been served. "We must have a proper one at Claydon as soon as it can be arranged."

"My grandmother has a suggestion," Harry offered. "Rather than your doing that—and reminding everyone of the past—she would like to hold a ball for Deirdre at Ainsworth Park."

Here was good news at last! Madge clapped her hands together in delight. "What a wonderful and generous idea!" she cried, beaming. Her dinner had become a success after all.

The next three days, however, were not a success. Harry had every intention of living up to his bargain, within limits. He would do all that was necessary, but not more. In that way, without actually *encouraging* Deirdre to find another flower in her garden of suitors, he would certainly do nothing to prevent it.

He called on his betrothed every day at midmorning and took her up in his curricle for a sedate drive through Bath's lovely curved streets and charming parks. If she requested his presence in the evenings, he dutifully presented himself. The first two evenings he managed to entice Charles into games of chess before Deirdre came down, and by the time Charles excused him from the chessboard, it was too late to go out. When it happened the second time, Deirdre became considerably annoyed. "This is too much inactivity, my love," she complained.

Harry, ever the gentleman, apologized. "I'm sorry, Deirdre. I fear you've attached yourself to a stodgy old stay-at-home. But please believe that I shall make every effort to change my ways, if it pleases you."

It pleased her to be taken to a dance at the Assembly Rooms that very night. Harry stood up with her for two dances, and she had willing partners for the others. One of those partners, a certain William Quiddington, was so taken with her melting eyes and golden tresses that he tripped over his feet and fell on his face, giving everyone in the room a reason to laugh and to cast admiring glances at the cause. The recipient of those admiring glances preened. She found the evening utterly delightful. She went home in the happiest of tempers.

But Harry was not one to miss an opportunity. The next day she received a note from him, expressing his regrets at the necessity of absenting himself from her. He had to go to London on urgent business, he wrote. He hoped he would not be gone for many days. A fortnight at the most.

Deirdre threw a tantrum. She stamped her feet, beat on the wall with her fists, and kicked over a pedestal, causing a crystal vase containing fresh flowers to crash to the floor. "How can he have left me like this?" she cried petulantly to her mother. "Here I am, on the first truly springlike day of the year, imprisoned at home with no escort, no amusements, and nobody to talk to!"

"You can come with me to the Pump Room," her mother suggested calmly.

"Oh, pooh! I dislike going to the Pump Room more than anything. Being forced to chat with a gaggle of old biddies is more than I should be expected to bear!"

But she did go to the Pump Room, and she was not forced to chat with a gaggle of old biddies. Instead, she came face to face with her admirer of the evening before—William Quiddington, Esquire. Within half an hour she was happily riding in his gig. And that very evening, she accepted his escort to a concert in the Upper Rooms. When her mother objected, she had an answer ready. "Just because Harry is not available does not mean I must suffer," she told her mother flatly. "We came here to Bath for the pleasures it offers, and I, for one, intend to enjoy them."

Charles saw nothing wrong in these arrangements, but Madge was no fool. It was plain to her that her daughter was not the most constant of females. If things were left as they were, the prospect of another broken betrothal loomed large.

But she need not have worried. Young William Quiddington was too eager a suitor. There was no challenge for Deirdre in capturing him, and she quickly became bored. If Harry had put any hope in the blooming of that particular flower, he was soon to learn it had shriveled.

When four days had passed without a sign of Harry's return, Madge decided to take matters into her own hands. "I think Deirdre and I should spend a few days in London," she told her husband. "We need to do some shopping for bride-clothes."

Charles was glad to let them go. They arrived in London at mid-afternoon, and as soon as they'd checked in at Fenton's Hotel, Madge went to call on her friend, Mrs. Compton, who knew everyone in London worth knowing. Mrs. Compton promptly procured for Lady Quigley and her party an invitation to a ball to be held that evening at Lady Landers' home. "It's for Gussie," Mrs. Compton informed her friend with a smirk. "She's found herself a beau at last. I think you may know him—Percival Greenway?"

The fact that Percy would be present at the affair did not trouble Madge. He would not be so foolish as to approach any of her party, but if he did, they had only to give him the cut direct. She promptly dismissed him from her mind.

With the invitation in her possession, Madge's next object was to let Harry know that she and Deirdre were in town and were expecting his escort that evening for the Landers' ball. *This will be Deirdre's first London ball, but she will have little pleasure in it if you are not with her*, she wrote in the missive she sent round to the Ainsworth town house.

Harry, hiding away in London to escape constraints of a betrothal not to his liking, should have been irritated by this peremptory summons from his mother-in-law-to-be. But in fact he was not at all perturbed. As he read the invitation, a smile slowly dawned in his eyes and soon spread over his entire face. He'd been spending his time making escape plans. This too-peremptory summons might fit into them perfectly.

When Madge read Harry's affirmative answer, a smile lit her face also. Even Harry was bound to be overwhelmed tonight, she thought, when he glimpsed her beautiful daughter bedecked in the magnificent ball gown Madge had brought for Deirdre to wear for just such an occasion.

Deirdre, under her mother's supervision, spent the rest of that afternoon and most of the evening preparing herself for the ball. Her abigail used the better part of two hours dressing her hair. It was curled and piled up atop her head, with one long, thick curl left hanging over her left shoulder. The gown Madge had chosen for her was a green Florentine silk, gathered tightly just under the bosom with a knot of white flowers, and then left to flow in graceful folds to the floor. It had short puffed sleeves that started well below the shoulder, leaving so low a décolletage that Deirdre herself was surprised. "You've told me time and time again that I'm too young to wear a gown cut so low," she said to her mother.

Madge shrugged. "You're betrothed now, so it's permitted."

At the appointed hour of nine, a footman appeared at the door of Madge's rooms and announced that a gentleman awaited them in the foyer downstairs.

Madge studied her daughter with a proud smile. Her eyes traveled from Deirdre's golden tresses, past her light-blue eyes (the lashes enhanced by just a touch of eye-blacking), past the swell of her breasts over the green silk bodice of her gown, past the slim waist and the elegant long white gloves, to the swirl of the full skirt. *If Harry doesn't lose his head over this vision*, Madge thought, *I know nothing of men*. "Go ahead and greet your Harry, my love," she ordered, smiling to herself at the prospect of the couple enjoying a romantic reunion alone together. "I'll follow shortly."

Deirdre, positively aglow, flew down the stairs to meet him.

There was no sign of Harry in the foyer. But after a few moments, a gentleman appeared from behind a pillar and came up to her. It was not Harry, but he was not a stranger, either. "Leonard?" she gasped, shocked.

"Good evening, my dear," Leonard said smoothly, lifting her gloved hand to his lips. "You look absolutely smashing!"

"Thank you," the bewildered girl murmured, "but where's Harry?"

"Harry had a minor injury to his leg and won't be able to dance tonight. He sent me to escort you in his place. I hope you won't mind. We can be partners for one evening, can't we? For old times' sake?"

Deirdre cocked her head, eyeing him carefully. With his wild red locks slicked back, his black coat fitting his broad shoulders and slim frame without a wrinkle, his white neckcloth folded into a perfect *trone d'amour,* and his red vest made even more dashing by the spectacular gold stripes, he looked complete to a shade. More impressive, perhaps, than Harry himself would have been. "Very well," she said, smiling and taking his arm. "For old times' sake."

THIRTY-SEVEN

When they arrived at the Landers' town house, Deirdre was surprised to see such a great crowd milling about the entrance. Carriages blocked the street in front of the house, and, inside, the stairway up to the ballroom was all but impassable. When she expressed her surprise to Leonard, he shrugged. "It's a typical London fête," he explained. "A London hostess doesn't consider her ball a success unless it's described as a crush."

When at last they made it to the top, a footman in full livery announced their arrival. "Madge, Lady Quigley," he intoned, "Miss Deirdre Quigley, and Sir Leonard Tyndale." Just inside the doorway, they passed along the receiving line consisting of Lady Landers, her elder daughter Emily, Emily's husband Sir Martin Redmond, and her younger daughter, Gussie. Madge gave Lady Landers a quick thank you for the invitation and passed on with just a nod to the elder daughter. But Emily caught her arm. "I say, Lady Madge," she whispered, "since Sir Leonard is with you, I suppose the rumors that your daughter is no longer attached to him are not true?"

"They are true," Madge said shortly, not pleased at what she felt was vulgar curiosity. "Leonard is merely escorting us tonight." And she walked on, coldly nodding to Emily's husband as she passed him. But she did take note of little Gussie. The girl was not beautiful, that much was true. Her nose was too prominent and her chin too receding. But there was a happy, excited glow about her this evening, which made her seem almost pretty. This surprised Madge. Gussie Landers did not look like the wallflower she'd been led to expect.

As the Quigley party passed on into the ballroom, Emily Redmond began to spread the news to every unmarried girl she greeted that the very attractive redheaded gentleman in the red-and-gold striped vest was unattached.

Deirdre expected to have her dance card filled in very short order, and she was not disappointed. What upset her, however, was the astounding number of gentlemen who came up to Leonard to introduce their daughters to him. Even before her own card was filled, Leonard was engaged for at least a dozen dances.

Madge watched her daughter step out on the dance floor for the first dance with Leonard and then took a seat on the sidelines. Not having forgotten that Percy was to be a guest, she kept a wary eye on the doorway, but the evening was well advanced before the footman announced "Sir Percival Greenway." Many an eye in addition to hers was attracted to his entrance, for he posed in the doorway for a long moment to give the assemblage the opportunity to admire him. He was indeed admirable, from the curls of his hair (some of them plastered firmly against his forehead) to the rosettes of his dancing shoes. The lapels of his evening coat were of velveret and wider than those of any other coat in the room. His shirtpoints reached up to his cheekbones, and, most remarkable of all, his waistcoat, cut stylishly short, had wide orange and yellow stripes and sported at least three fobs hanging by ribbons from the pockets. "Will you look at that cock-of-the game?" Madge heard a gentleman sitting behind her remark sardonically. "Nugee, who outfits all the young fools these days, seems to have outdone himself this time."

It belatedly occurred to Madge that she should perhaps have warned Leonard and her daughter that Percy would be present this evening. She turned nervously on her chair and searched the crowd to see if she could spot them, but she could not.

Deirdre was dancing with a round-faced young gentleman who was awestruck at her fairy-princess beauty. That awe made him tongue-tied, an affliction that troubled a number of the young men she met. Tongue-tied partners were not particularly interesting to her, so when she became aware of a slight commotion in the crowd and saw Lady Landers hurry across the floor to greet someone, she turned her head to see who had caused the stir. "Oh, my heavens!" she exclaimed aloud. "It's Percy!"

"What did you say?" her partner asked.

"Oh! Nothing," Deirdre mumbled and tried to keep her mind on the dance. But she could not. She couldn't help glancing over her shoulder toward Leonard. She knew just where to find him; curious to see how he reacted to each of his partners, she'd kept a sharp eye on him all evening. She saw at once that he'd recognized the new arrival. His look of surprise was immediately overtaken with one of fury. As Deirdre watched, Leonard made a bow to his partner and left her standing deserted in the middle of the floor. *Dear God*, Deirdre prayed, *don't let him make a scene!*

The movement of the dance forced her to turn away. When she was able to look back, she saw that Leonard had already reached Percy's side. Percy's face paled to an ashen hue and, as if under a spell, he allowed Leonard take his arm and lead him away from his hostess and across the floor. Deirdre, knowing Leonard had somehow coerced Percy to walk off with him, could not bear to continue dancing. "Please excuse me, sir," she said to her bewildered partner, "but I must leave. There's a young lady standing not to far away behind you who would be most grateful, I'm sure, to take my place and finish the dance with you." And blundering through the startled dancers, she made her way off the dance floor.

Leonard was pushing the ashen-faced Percy out a side door. Deirdre restrained herself from running after them, for she did not want to attract any more notice than she already had. She walked purposefully but at a dignified pace to the side door, opened it, and found herself on a terrace surrounded by a stone balustrade. Leonard, clutching Percy by his neckcloth, had backed him against one of the balustrade's posts and was preparing to take a swing at him. "Leonard, don't!" Percy was begging, holding up a hand to protect his jaw. "Haven't you done enough to my poor face?"

"Not by a long shot, you clunch!" Leonard said with enraged relish. "Did you think that merely one blow was enough to make me forgive what you did to Deirdre?" He pulled back his arm and readied himself to swing.

"No, Leonard, please!" Deirdre cried.

Leonard looked over his shoulder at her. "Go back inside, Deirdre," he ordered. "Stay out of this. I was afraid I'd never have the chance to let him feel my fives, but now that I have, I intend to make good use of the opportunity."

"No, don't let him hit me, Deirdre," Percy pleaded. "At least, not yet."

"What do you mean, not yet?" Leonard barked. "Do you expect me to let you make an escape, as you did from Bath when you knew I'd be coming after you?"

"I won't escape from here," Percy said. "I did a fool thing abducting Deirdre. I admit that. I know I deserve a proper beating. But if you would only wait a bit—"

"Why on earth would I be idiot enough to wait a bit?"

"You see," Percy mumbled, rubbing his jaw tenderly, "I wouldn't want them to see me all mauled about."

"You mean, you don't want to be seen with your foppish shirtpoints all wilted and your neckcloth bloody," Leonard sneered.

"No, I don't," Percy admitted in a plaintive whine. "And you know how my jaw swells up. How will that look when they announce my betrothal in half an hour?"

Leonard lowered his arm. "What balderdash is this?"

"It ain't balderdash. Lady Landers is going to announce it right before the doors open for the buffet. Positively!"

"I don't believe a word of this. You'd say anything to keep from—"

But Deirdre cut him off. "Wait a moment, Leonard. Let him speak. Are you saying, Percy, that you're going to be married?" Her eyes widened with sudden understanding. "Good heavens! Not to Gussie Landers?"

"Yes, to Gussie Landers," Percy muttered defensively. "Why not?"

Leonard turned to Deirdre in amused surprise. "Is that the chit with no chin?"

"She may not be a beauty like Deirdre," Percy said angrily, "but she's pretty enough for me. At least she's completely devoted to me and won't be falling in love with every man who passes by, like some females I know."

Leonard wheeled round to him furiously. "Apologize for that slur, you bobbing-block!"

Deirdre put up her chin. "Never mind, Leonard. Percy has good reason for what he said. And, Percy, I'm sure Gussie's a fine young woman, and I hope you'll be very happy. Let him go, Leonard. Under the circumstances, we can put the mistakes of the past behind us."

"As you say, my dear," Leonard agreed, finding his anger dissipated by this turn of events. "Go on, old man, to your betrothal announcement." He patted down Percy's disordered neckcloth and pushed him back toward the door. "I'll even wish you well."

After Percy scurried off, Leonard, about to offer his arm to Deirdre to take her back inside, noticed that she was gazing up at him with a strange expression. "What is it, my dear?" he asked in concern.

"It's you," she said, remembering a bit ruefully that he was no longer her betrothed. "You are so . . . so heroic. Positively!"

THIRTY-EIGHT

❧

The invitation came at last. Isabel read it over several times, although the message was perfectly clear: The pleasure of their company was requested for a costume ball to be held at Ainsworth Park, Surrey, on Saturday, the fifteenth of April at nine in the evening. An additional card was enclosed in the beige-colored vellum envelope, giving the information that, as family members and close friends, their presence would be welcomed during the week preceding the event, and that a response giving the date and time of their arrival would be appreciated. Scrawled at the bottom in a less formal hand than the invitation itself were the words *Remember your promise! L. A.*

Isabel had to screw up her courage to bring up the subject with her daughter. She waited until the next morning, after Kate had returned, rosy-cheeked and invigorated, from a brisk canter on her favorite mare.

Isabel read the invitation aloud, putting into her tone of voice all the enthusiasm she could muster. But it was to no avail. Kate didn't even let her finish. "Surely, Mama, you don't expect me to go!" she said at once.

"You *must* go," Isabel insisted. "Lady Ainsworth would be dreadfully offended if you refused. Your aunt and uncle are surely counting on our presence, and Deirdre would be devastated if you were absent."

"I don't care. My aunt and uncle won't miss me, and as for Deirdre, she will have a great deal to make her happy. If she feels any disappointment about my not being there, it will be too small a pain to be noticed amid all that joy."

"Kate Rendell!" her mother scolded. "I've never known you to be so . . . so unfeeling!"

"I'm a sour old maid, just as you said," the daughter retorted, "and as such, I'm entitled to my crotchets."

"No, you're not. There is no entitlement to selfishness!"

Kate was taken aback. "Selfishness? Is it selfish to wish to protect myself against the pain I will surely suffer if I attend?" She turned her back on her mother and strode angrily toward the door. "One would think my own mother would concern herself with her daughter's feelings instead of her niece's."

"But what about my feelings?" Isabel asked.

Kate paused. "Yours?"

"Yes, mine. Edward will be there, you know. And I have every reason to believe he plans to use that occasion to make me an offer."

"Mama!" Kate flew back across the room and gave her mother an ecstatic embrace. "How wonderful! I've been hoping it would happen."

"Really, Kate?" She backed away in order to search her daughter's face. "Do you like him? Truly?"

"Like him? I adore him! He's perfect for you."

"I'm so glad." She was indeed glad that her daughter approved of Edward, but this was not the time to celebrate. She had to convince her daughter to accept the invitation by any means she could devise. Therefore, she let her face fall and her shoulders droop. "I suppose there'll be some other occasion for Edward to declare himself," she said with a melodramatic tremor.

Kate was not fooled. "Oh, very well, Mama," she said, elbows akimbo. "You needn't overdo it. You've won me over. I'll go."

Isabel smiled in triumph. "Thank you, my love," she sighed in relief, and she placed a kiss on Kate's cheek.

"But not for the entire week," Kate bargained. "Tell her ladyship we'll arrive only the day before the ball. Two days will be torture enough for me."

Isabel, grateful for that much, quickly agreed.

Kate started out of the room again. "One more thing," she said over her shoulder. "I shan't bother about a costume. A half-mask will be enough for me."

"Don't be silly, Isabel said. "I've been making something for you for months. It's the perfect costume." She went to the sofa and pulled her embroidery cart forward. "Come and see."

"Something you've embroidered?" Kate asked,

coming back into the room. "Are you planning to costume me as a sofa cushion?"

Isabel didn't deign to reply. She merely took some pins from the finished part of her work that was rolled at the bottom of the embroidery frame and let it fall free. Kate gasped. It was an exact copy of the shawl in the painting. Every detail—the rich blue background; the silver, red, and green leaves, striated with lines of orange and purple; the filligreed design of the border—all perfectly replicated in a work of stunning richness. "Oh, Mama!" Kate breathed, almost speechless.

Isabel beamed. "There's your costume, my love. You shall go as the girl in the Persian shawl."

THIRTY-NINE

❧❧❧

Kate had to hold herself back from hanging out the window of the carriage as it rode up the tree-lined approach to Ainsworth Park. She wanted to see everything. Her first view of the estate was breathtaking. There was an air of spaciousness and timelessness about the place, and when she compared it with Rendell Hall it made her sigh. The Hall was old and dark, like an old abbey. Here the grounds were sunny and well-kept, and the sweep of lawn drew one's eyes to the house itself, a beautiful white building with a high, pedimented entrance at the center of a wide façade, its extended line broken by tall, symmetrically spaced, sparkling windows. Even Claydon Castle, large and impressive as it was, could not compare to the gracious Palladian elegance of this.

As soon as the carriage drew to a stop, two footmen came running down the stone staircase to help the ladies alight. They were immediately followed by Lady Ainsworth and Harry. Lady Ainsworth gave Kate a warm embrace and an enthusiastic welcome, while Harry did the same to Isabel. Kate grew tense as Harry turned to her, but the awkwardness of facing him was eased by a shout from the top of the stairs. "Kate, Kate, you're here!" It was Benjy. He came hurtling down the steps, and, with boyish eagerness, thrust himself in front of his brother and enveloped Kate in an affectionate hug.

"Benjy! Your arm!" Kate cautioned, laughing.

"His arm is quite healthy," Harry said, drily. "I wish I could say the same about his manners."

Lady Ainsworth took Isabel's arm and started up the steps that led to the colonnaded landing in front of the entrance. Harry was about to do the same for Kate, but his brother was quicker. Benjy took hold of her arm and led her toward the steps. "Because of you, I've learned to dance," he confided to her, ignoring his brother who was helplessly following them, "so I want you to promise to let me stand up with you at the dance tomorrow."

Kate, wondering if Harry was still concerned about his brother's youthful infatuation with her, cast him a questioning glance over her shoulder. Harry, with an amused smile, merely shrugged. "I'd be delighted to dance with you," she told Benjy.

"Splendid," the boy crowed. "For the quadrille? I know the steps. And for a country dance, too?"

"No," Harry said, ruffling the boy's hair, "I draw the line at country dances. One dance is all I'll permit, even if the lady is willing. Even one is more than an unmannerly schoolboy deserves."

"Speaking of school," Kate observed as they reached the landing, "shouldn't you be there?"

"Harry let me come home for this occasion," the boy explained.

"And this is the thanks I get," Harry put in. "You haven't let me get in a word of greeting to our guest."

"Never mind," Benjy retorted. "You'll have plenty of time to speak to her later. I want to ask her to let me escort her in to dinner tonight."

"Now, that, Benjamin Gerard," his brother said with mock severity, "is the outside of enough. We have a houseful of guests, all of whom have a greater right to that honor than you."

"Oh, pooh!" Kate laughed. "Of course you may escort me, Benjy."

Harry gave her a glinting look before turning to his brother. "Very well, you've won that point," he said, giving him a light shove in the direction of the door. "Now take yourself off and don't let me see that grinning face of yours until dinnertime."

Benjy threw Kate a triumphant wave and ran off. Harry, with a sigh of relief, took her hands in his. "At last I can have a moment to speak to—"

A cry from just inside the door stopped him. "Kate, my dearest, I've been waiting and waiting!" cried Deirdre, who, with her skirts lifted, came running toward them.

"Blast!" Harry cursed under his breath. "Not another interruption."

Deirdre took no notice. She embraced her cousin with breathless eagerness. "You've no idea how long I've been waiting at the window for you," she exclaimed. "I don't see why you couldn't come days ago!"

"Well, you see, I—" Kate began.

"Never mind. You're here now. Come and take a walk with me, dearest. I must talk to you."

Harry felt he had to interfere, if only as a good host. "Don't you think you might wait until Kate has had a moment to refresh herself?" he asked.

Deirdre would not be deterred. "You can spare me a few moments, can't you, Kate?" And without waiting for an answer, she drew her cousin toward the staircase. "You needn't wait for us, Harry," she threw back over her shoulder. "As soon as we've talked, I'll show Kate to her room myself."

Keeping a close grip on Kate's arm, Deirdre pulled her cousin down the steps and along the path that edged the house until they were hidden behind a patch of shrubbery. "You've got to help me, Kate," she said, her voice trembling.

Kate, who'd found Deirdre's greeting irksome enough, was quite out of patience. "What is it now, Deirdre?" she asked, trying to curb her irritation.

"It's this betrothal," Deirdre said. "I don't want to go through with it."

"*What?*" Kate could not believe her ears. "Why ever not?"

"Because I don't love Harry after all."

"Don't love him?" Kate glared at her in disgust.

"Didn't you tell me he was the most handsome and the most charming and the most witty and all the other 'mosts' of all the men you'd ever met?"

Deirdre wrung her hands. "I might have done. But I'm afraid I've . . . I've changed my mind."

"How can you possibly have changed your mind?"

"Because he's a bore!"

"A bore? *Harry?*" Kate rolled her eyes heavenward. "You've lost your mind!"

"You don't know him as I do. All he likes to do is play chess or read the *Times* or ride about in his stodgy old curricle that doesn't even have a high perch!"

"If it's high-perched vehicles you wanted, you should have stayed betrothed to Percy," Kate snapped. At the thought of Percy, suddenly the purpose of this conversation burst upon her. "There's someone else, isn't there?" she asked in revulsion. "You've taken a fancy to someone new!"

Deirdre dropped her eyes. "Not exactly."

"What do you mean, 'not exactly'?"

"It's not someone new. It's Leonard. He's the one I truly love."

"Are you telling me," Kate demanded furiously, "that you want to jilt Harry for Leonard?"

Deirdre tried not to be frightened by Kate's fury. "Yes, I do," she said, putting up her chin bravely. "And I want you to tell Harry for me."

Kate stared at her for a few moments, openmouthed. Then she grasped her cousin by the shoulders and gave her a shaking. "Listen to me, Deirdre, and listen well. You will *not* jilt Harry! You made a promise to him, and you're going to keep it! He cares for you, and I will not have him hurt, do you hear me? *I will not have him hurt!*"

"Kate!" Deirdre gaped at her hitherto-affectionate cousin in alarmed amazement. "What's wrong with you?"

"Never mind what's wrong with me," Kate said between clenched teeth. "I'm warning you, Deirdre, that if you so much as *hint* to anyone that you are not delighted to become Harry's bride, I will tell Leonard and every man you meet what a capricious, faithless, rattlepate you are, and I shall never, *never* speak to you again as long as I live!" And, shoving the astounded Deirdre away from her, she turned and stalked off.

On the landing directly above them, Harry wanted to dance a jig in glee. He'd been eavesdropping, and every word he'd overheard had pleased him. The words couldn't have been more perfect for his plans if he'd composed those speeches himself.

FORTY

❧

As soon as Kate had settled into her room and changed from her traveling clothes, she came downstairs to look for Lady Ainsworth. She found her hostess in one of the sitting rooms, drinking tea with Madge, Charles, and Sir Edward. "Come in, Kate, and join us," Lady Ainsworth said. "I've asked the younger set to join us for tea, but they seem to be scattered all about, doing whatever you young people like to do. If you'd like to be with them, you'll probably find them wandering about the grounds or at the stable arranging for riding. Would you like to take tea with us or go searching for them?"

"What I'd really like to do, your ladyship," Kate admitted, "is to find my way to the library to see that painting you told me of."

"Is that the painting Harry was seeking when he first

appeared at Rendell Hall?" Madge asked. "If it is, I, too, should like to see it."

"Then why don't we all go," Lady Ainsworth suggested. "I'd be delighted to show it to you all. I'm so very proud of it."

They all very willingly got to their feet and followed their hostess down the hall. The library was so large a room that it required three chandeliers to hang from its high ceiling. Four tall windows filled the south-facing wall. The walls to the right and left of it were completely covered with shelves filled with books, and the wall opposite held an enormous stone fireplace. Over it, in a place of honor, hung the portrait in an elaborate gilded frame. The late-afternoon sunlight, slanting in from the windows, threw its rays just where they were wanted—right on the portrait. Lady Ainsworth led her guests to the center of the room. "There she is," she announced, pointing. "*The Girl in White.*"

There was a large chorus of *aaaahs*. "Lovely," Sir Edward said.

"A charming piece of work," Charles agreed.

Kate, though saying nothing, couldn't help studying the painting more critically than the others. She was comparing it to that other painting she knew so well— *Girl with Persian Shawl.* The subject matter of the two paintings was indeed similar—a smiling girl in a white dress against a background of greenery—but the quality of the work was very different. This girl wore a light pelisse of a simple blue satin rather than a shawl, for one thing, and it had nothing like the subtlety of detail and the glowing colors of the Persian shawl. But there were other differences, too. Where the artist of the Persian shawl painting had, with a firm hand, made a brave show of contrasts, this artist seemed somewhat timid. The colors were pale, and the brush strokes wavered. Even in the fabric of the gowns, the difference was apparent. One could almost touch the fabric of the first, whereas in the second, the gown was a white blur. But what was most fascinating to Kate were the faces. *The Girl in White* was apparently posing for the artist with a forced smile, whereas the *Girl with Persian Shawl* looked as if she'd been caught unawares. That detail alone made Kate believe that the painter of this portrait was an amateur. He had not the confidence and talent that were apparent in the Persian shawl work.

Of course, Harry had admitted that his artist-ancestor was an amateur. He and his grandmother were not seeking a work of art but a portrait of a kinswoman. And Kate had to admit that the girl in this painting was prettier. She was fair-haired and light-eyed, and she gazed in wide-eyed adoration on all who looked at her. One could never take a dislike to such a sweetly innocuous face, the way one could toward the arrogant girl in the Persian shawl.

Charles was studying the painting, too. "I don't see any signature," he remarked. "How did Harry know this was the right one?"

"He had a very detailed description. I don't think there's any doubt of its authenticity," Lady Ainsworth said complacently.

"Do you know what I think?" Madge exclaimed in

delight. "I think she looks a little like Deirdre!"

Lady Ainsworth cocked her head and gazed at the portrait through narrowed eyes. "I hadn't thought of that before," she said, "but now that you mention it, I can see a slight resemblance."

Of course there's a resemblance, Kate thought. *Harry must have seen it at once, and that's why he decided it was the work he was seeking. Love makes one blind.*

Lady Ainsworth turned to Kate. "Well, my love, now that you've seen it, what do you think?"

"I think the girl is very pretty," she said. "Far prettier than the girl in the painting Harry wanted to buy from me."

Just down the hall, in a small sitting room, Leonard discovered Deirdre curled up in an armchair, her shoulders shaking. The tremors were caused by her attempt to keep the sobs that were filling her chest from bursting out of her. After all, it would not do for the affianced bride of the host of this party to be discovered weeping on the day before the official announcement of their intended nuptials. If Kate, for one, found her like this, she might very well give her another shaking.

Leonard came up to her, knelt down, and reached for the hand that was covering her face. "What's the trouble, little girl?" he asked softly.

She buried her head deeper into the back of the chair. "I c-can't tell you," she said, a bubble of tears in her mouth.

"Then let me tell you. You don't want to go through with the betrothal, but you're afraid to admit it."

She lifted her head and gazed at him wide-eyed. "How d-did you know?"

"I know you, Deirdre. You can't seem to stay in love with anyone for very long."

"That's v-very unkind of you," she said, pouting. "Are you going to c-call me a capricious, f-faithless, rattlep-pate, as Kate did?"

"No, of course not. But you must admit that you've been behaving in a manner that any objective observer might consider faithless and rattlepated."

"I suppose they might," she admitted. "But Leonard, there is one thing in my favor.

"Oh? And what is that?"

She leaned toward him with a tremulous smile, "I always seem to c-come b-back to you in the end."

"As now?" he asked.

"Yes, as now." She looked at him pleadingly. "You do believe that it's you I love, don't you?"

"I believe that you do at this moment."

"Always, I swear it!" She tried to embrace him. "I do truly love you so!"

"You've said those words to me before," he said, holding her back. "Before Harry, and before Percy, and before Harry again. Who, I wonder, is coming next?"

"No one, I promise! Please, Leonard, believe me. I've never loved anyone as I do you."

"I wish I could believe you, Deirdre. I love you to

distraction, you know, even when you're a capricious rattlepate."

Overjoyed at those words, she threw her arms about his neck. "Then my dearest," she asked hopefully, "will you be my betrothed again?"

"I hope so," was his calm response. "Some day."

"Some day?" Her lips began to tremble again. "What do you mean?"

"I mean, my love, that I will be your faithful suitor, as I always have been, for one more year. If at the end of the time, you have managed to avoid tumbling top-over-tail for another man, I shall offer for you again. But if you should be tempted even once to turn your thoughts in another direction, you'll see the last of me."

She opened her mouth to argue, but she closed it again. After the muddle she'd made with her foolish infatuations, she had to admit that his decision was reasonable. "Oh, very well," she sighed. "Now, stop looking so stern and kiss me."

"No, you must do something first. You must tell Harry the truth."

She snuggled close to him and fingered his neck-cloth. "Can't you do it for me?"

"No! You must behave like a grown-up, sensible woman and tell him yourself."

"All right, I will. When?"

"Right now!"

FORTY-ONE

❧

On the morning of the day of the costume ball, the house guests woke to the sound of torrential rain. This did not trouble the women, all of whom intended to spend the day indoors anyway. It would take them all day to ready themselves for the evening. There was so much for them to do—last-minute adjustments to their costumes; designing and redesigning their hairstyles to conform to their chosen roles; bathing in a tin tub, for which one waited one's turn, as the harried house-maids had to drag the tubs from room to room; applying lotions and ointments to arms and faces; and, when all that was accomplished, painting their faces white, blacking their lashes and eyebrows with burnt ivory sticks, and applying reddened lip salve to their mouths. Only then would they begin to dress.

For the men, the rain was a greater annoyance. Because their costumes were simpler—most choosing merely to wear loosely fitted, hooded dominoes over their evening clothes—costume preparation was much less time-consuming for them. Thus, free of the constraints of women and time, the men had planned a hunting party for the day. The heavy rain made that excursion impossible. They were forced to amuse themselves with the milder diversions of piquet and whist.

Fortunately, by nine in the evening, the rain had stopped. The guests who were arriving by carriage could emerge and climb the steps without fear that their costumes would be soaked. The grand ballroom began to fill. Soon the glinting lights of hundreds of candles sparkled on a colorful display of fifty masked revelers. Among them were several Marie Antoinettes, at least three pantalooned harem women, a good number of clowns and harlequins, an African princess, and one well-stuffed, hairy brown bear complete with a lifelike head.

Sir Edward had not told Isabel what he would wear. She hadn't told him, either. Since she'd been busy putting finishing touches on the magnificent Persian shawl, she didn't decide until late in the afternoon what her own costume would be. In a last-minute inspiration, she chose to dress herself in Edward's own fashion. She strapped her bosom flat and covered it with a starched shirt and neckcloth borrowed from the butler. Then she put on a red vest, a pair of black knee britches, a wide-cuffed coat, and a powdered peruke tied back with a black ribbon. These were all borrowed from Charles, except the wig, which the ingenious butler had managed to procure for her.

After she'd dressed, she looked at herself in the mirror. Though her face was still womanly, the rest of her looked properly masculine. Pleased with herself, she took up a cane (also borrowed from Charles) in one hand, a lacy handkerchief in the other, and sauntered across the hall in the mincing manner of an eighteenth-century dandy to show her manly costume to her daughter.

Kate took one look at her transformed mother and hooted with laughter. Isabel looked down at her plump stomach buttoned tightly into the red vest and joined in. A moment later, however, her laughter died. "Am I too shocking, dressed as a man?" she asked.

"I think you're adorable," Kate said when she'd caught her breath. "But, Mama, is it possible that Edward will think you're making fun of him?"

Isabel hadn't thought of that possibility, but after considering it, she only shrugged. "I refuse to worry about that," she said airily. "If he doesn't have a sense of humor, I don't want him. Come now, let's get you into your gown."

A few moments later, Kate herself was transformed. Like the girl in the portrait, her dark hair was piled up on her head, with a profusion of short curls left loose to frame her face, the soft white gown fell in folds from a high, gathered waist, and the ornately embroidered shawl fell over one shoulder and was draped over the other arm. Isabel clasped her hands to her flattened breast and sighed in pleasure. "I've never seen you look so beautiful!" she exclaimed.

"Are you admiring me or your handiwork?" Kate teased.

"You're both my handiwork," Isabel retorted.

"I suppose that's true," Kate sighed as they started out, "but there are fewer flaws in the shawl."

Isabel didn't answer. She was thinking, with growing alarm, of what Edward might feel when he saw her dressed this way. She had not meant the costume to make a mock of him, but he might very well see it that way. She walked out of the room and down the stairs with a queasy feeling in her chest. She didn't like the feeling at all. *Isabel Rendell*, she scolded herself, *you're supposed to be serene!*

Kate also started down the stairs with a knot of misery in her chest. For the second time in a few short months, she would have to endure hearing the announcement of Harry's betrothal to her cousin. It was bad enough that first time, when Harry had been no more than a figment of her daydreams. This time it would be infinitely worse. *Damnation,* she swore under her breath, *why did I ever come?*

In the crowd that milled about at the entrance to the ballroom, Kate and her mother became separated. Kate, gazing about with fascination at the splendor of jewels and the dazzle of colors around her, blundered into Deirdre. The two young women eyed each other awkwardly, Kate still angry and Deirdre filled with guilt. "Good evening, Kate," Deirdre said. "I love your costume. You're the Persian shawl painting, aren't you?"

Kate had to smile, "And you're the painting in the library! You look as lovely as she."

And indeed she did. In the soft white gown with the blue pelisse, and with her golden hair left to fall in natural simplicity, Deirdre's face shone with its innate sweetness.

"You look lovely, too," Deirdre said hastily, and, not wishing to answer any questions that might lead Kate to guess that she'd broken off with Harry, she turned and disappeared into the throng.

Kate gazed after her, brow wrinkled. Beyond her embarrassment, Deirdre seemed to be radiating happiness. Why? Did she decide she wanted the betrothal after all? Had Harry done or said something to make her fall in love with him again? He was quite capable of winning back her affections, Kate was sure of that.

At that moment, a pirate with a huge painted *mustachio* over his lip bowed before her. "The music is about to begin," he said in a growling voice. "By my sword, I demand the right to stand up with you."

The tricorne he wore, with a skull-and-bones painted on it, made the pirate look almost as tall as Kate, but she was not fooled. She laughed. "Of course, Denjy. Didn't I promise it to you?"

"You look smashing," he said to her with boyish enthusiasm.

"So do you. Quite a convincing cutthroat. I hope you won't make me walk the plank."

He led her to the dance floor. Kate soon discovered that he'd mastered the steps of the quadrille quite well. She was truly enjoying herself until they broke apart for movement of the dance, when she caught a glimpse of Deirdre, dancing with a knight in full armor and gazing up at him with adoration. The knight was Leonard, of course. Kate bit her lip in concern. What was that little minx up to?

Meanwhile, Isabel discovered Edward standing in the far corner of the ballroom, scanning the crowd. To her surprise, he was dressed in the same manner as she: old-fashioned coat, knee britches, and powdered hair. He'd evidently felt that his eighteenth-century garb was costume enough. She adjusted her mask and, swinging her cane and handkerchief, strutted right past him. He barely took notice. She minced past him again, this time raising her handkerchief and brushing it against his cheek. He looked up after her, eyebrows raised in annoyance, but it wasn't until she turned her face toward him that he gasped in recognition. "Isabel! Good heavens!" And he broke into a spasm of laughter.

She came up to him, smiling broadly. "We seem to be of the same mind," she chortled. "We might pass for twins, if I were slimmer."

"No," he said, "you've too pretty a face to be my twin. But we might pass for brothers."

Isabel took his arm. "Would it be possible for brothers to dance together?"

"We'll surely raise a few eyebrows," he answered, leading her to the dance floor, "but I don't care."

• • •

The evening was well advanced when Harry, dressed casually in a domino that he hadn't even bothered to close over his evening clothes, found his way to Kate's side. He took off his mask so that he might get a better look at her. "Good God!" he said admiringly, "you're the portrait to the life!"

"If you remember what you said when you first saw the portrait, my lord, you will realize that is not a compliment," Kate pointed out.

"If I said anything other than 'the girl is lovely,' I have no recollection of it."

"You said she looked arrogant," Kate reminded him.

"Ah, but you knew I lied. You accused me of belittling the work to get a lower price."

She lowered her head. "Yes, I did. I'm sorry. I did not then . . . know you."

Harry grinned broadly. "Well, well, do I hear an apology from the oh-so-strong-minded Miss Rendell? I am overwhelmed. Shall we celebrate by standing up for the next dance?"

She took his arm, and they joined the couples on the floor. "Lovely as you are, Kate, draped in that magnificent shawl," he said as they took their place, "your mother and Sir Edward are outshining you. Everyone is smiling at the sight of them."

"Yes," Kate said as they parted for a figure. "Tweedledum and Tweedledee."

When they came together again, Kate broached the subject of Deirdre. "Your affianced bride has brought *your* painting to life. And very beautifully."

"My affianced bride is not—" Harry began, but the movement of the danced separated them again. By the time they came together again, it was time for the final bow. Harry took her arm to lead her off the floor. "As I was saying, my affianced bride—" he began again.

This time, a Marie Antoinette bedecked in jewels and a feathered headdress on her high pompadour pulled his arm from Kate's. "My dance, my lord, I believe," she said in queenly fashion and dragged him off. Harry could only throw Kate a helpless look before disappearing into the throng.

She did not see him again until midnight. When the clock struck the hour, he appeared on the musician's platform and announced the unmasking. This was done with appropriately noisy squeals of surprise and laughter. When the din subsided he cleared his throat. "I think it's time," he said, "for me to tell you why we've invited you all to celebrate with us tonight."

The throng surged forward to hear him.

"You all seem to be under the impression that I'm about to announce a betrothal. But that is not the case. There is no betrothal to be announced."

"Yes, there is," came a voice from the crowd.

Harry squinted into the press of people. "Sir Edward, is that you?"

"Yes, it is." The crowd parted as he pushed his way to the front, pulling Isabel behind him. "I'd like to announce to the world that this lovely lady in men's clothing has just consented to become my wife."

Isabel, as surprised as everyone else by this public proclamation, blushed hotly. "It's because we look so much alike," she muttered with an embarrassed laugh.

An enthusiastic cheer went up from the crowd, as Edward, emboldened by her acceptance of his proposal, embraced her. On her part, Isabel was suddenly shy. Undone by so much attention, she buried her head in his shoulder. "Take me out of here," she whispered in his ear, "or I shall die of embarrassment. This is not a proper way for me to maintain my serenity."

Everyone's eyes followed them as Edward led her out, but as soon as they disappeared, the audience turned back to Harry. Kate, standing at the back, was beset with a confusion of emotions. She was happy for her mother and wanted to run after the pair to wish them well. But she could not move. She had to hear what else Harry would say. What had he meant when he said there would be no betrothal? Had her selfish minx of a cousin broken it off? That possibility was so upsetting she could hardly breathe.

"Happy as I am at the news we've just heard," Harry was saying, "that was not the reason for this celebration. The reason is a birthday. A very special birthday. My grandmother, Charlotte, Lady Ainsworth, was born on this day seventy-five years ago."

Cheers rang through the room. Harry held up a hand for quiet. "You are all invited to go downstairs, drink to her health, and partake of a midnight supper. I've asked the youngest member of the family to lead the oldest down. Benjy, do the honors."

Benjy threw aside his pirate hat and, grinning proudly, gave his arm to his grandmother. The crowd made an aisle for them and applauded loudly as he led her out.

While the revelers gaily followed, Kate stood still, her chest tight with fury. Her eyes scanned the crowd for Deirdre. It didn't take long to find her, for the irritating chit was hanging on to the arm of a tall knight who could not be missed. Kate pushed her way through the press until she reached her target. Disentangling the girl's arm from Leonard's, Kate asked with restrained fury, "You will excuse us for a moment, won't you, Leonard?"

Not waiting for an answer she pushed Deirdre before her to the part of the ballroom that was now deserted. "Blast you, Deirdre," she snapped, "what did you do?"

Deirdre's underlip trembled. "About what?" she asked fearfully.

"You know about what! About Harry!"

Deirdre put up her chin. "I told him the truth. It was the right thing to do. Leonard said so."

"Did he, indeed?" Kate asked icily. "Tell me, Deirdre, why is it that Harry's best friend and the girl he saved from abduction both can care so little for his happiness?"

"I don't see what business it is of yours," Deirdre said with a pout. "Besides, it seems to me—"

Leonard came up behind her and put a protective arm about her shoulders. "I think, Kate," he said, "that Harry is not so very unhappy as you think." With that, Deirdre's knight took his lady's arm and led her toward the door. But before leaving he looked back at

Kate with a strange, enigmatic smile. "If I were you," he called back to her, "I'd take myself to the library."

"What?" Kate asked. "Why?"

Leonard pointed to his left. "The library," he repeated and disappeared.

Kate knew she should go down to the buffet and congratulate her mother and new father, but first she had to find out what Leonard was trying to tell her. She made her way to the library with hurried steps. When she opened the door, she was only half surprised to see Harry sitting there, sunk in an armchair with his feet up on an ottoman, his hands behind his head, staring up at the portrait of the Deirdre-like girl. Her heart went out to him. Perhaps Leonard, even though a rival for Deirdre's hand, was still Harry's friend and, guessing he'd be sitting here moping, had sent her here to try to console him.

She came in quietly and went to stand behind his chair. "You may not think so now," she said softly, "but there are many other girls in the world as lovely as she."

Harry turned his head and looked up at her. "Are there, indeed? Do you advise me to start right out and go looking for one of them?"

There was something so sarcastic in his tone that she was taken aback. "I don't . . . I didn't mean . . ."

"Do you really think, Miss Closed-minded Rendell, that I was sitting here mooning over that painting? Or the girl in it?"

"Weren't you?"

"No, ma'am, I was not. I don't even like it. Or her, for that matter."

"You don't like the painting that you traveled so many miles to purchase?" she asked. Her heart began to pound, but she wasn't sure why.

"I bought it for Grandmama. It means something to her. Family history or some such rot. My taste in paintings runs to a different sort of work."

"Does it?" she asked in a tiny voice. "And your taste in girls, too?"

He got to his feet and turned to her. "Dash it, Kate, I don't understand what crotchets you manufacture in your maggotty little brain. Didn't you hear me tell you, at the inn that night, that it was you I loved?"

Kate gulped. "You never told me that."

"Not in so many words, perhaps, but what else could I have meant when I said it was you I'd come to rescue?"

"You might have tried to rescue any female, just because you are kind and courageous."

"Kind and courageous, am I?" he sneered. "In addition to being a rake?"

"I may have been wrong about that," she admitted.

"You may have been wrong about a great deal. How can you possibly have taken it into your head that I loved Deirdre, when you were witness to the agony I felt that night?"

"But if you didn't love her, why didn't you tell her so? Why didn't you try to convince Leonard to take your place?"

"Because, my dear blockhead, it is not easy to reject

a young lady when she throws herself into your arms with deep expressions of love and gratitude. What I've been doing these last weeks, with Leonard's help, is trying to encourage Deirdre to reject me."

"Oh!" Kate breathed, wide-eyed.

"You could have spoilt everything, you know, when you threatened her yesterday, demanding that she stay faithful to me. Touched as I was by your concern for my happiness, I would have run downstairs and wrung your neck, except that I knew she would not follow your orders."

"You heard me?"

"Every word. Actually, you were magnificent." He took hold of the two ends of the shawl in a tight grip and used them to pull her to him. "So, girl in the Persian shawl, have I managed to convince you that I love you madly?"

"Do you? Arrogant and stubborn and closed-minded and blockheaded though I am?"

"That's why it's madly." Keeping her tied to him with the shawl, he leaned down and kissed her with the intensity of a desire long delayed. Slowly, she inched her arms free of the constraints and wound them round his neck. Locked that way in each other's arms, the shawl was no longer needed. It slipped quietly to the floor.

When at last they stopped for breath, he bent down and picked it up. "It's an amazing piece of work," he said in a choked voice. "I almost can't believe it's real. I almost can't believe *you're* real."

"Come now, Harry, whatever you feel now is not

what you felt when you first saw the painting," Kate said, taking the shawl and smoothing it out. "You can't make me believe that you admired it when you saw it that first day,"

"Oh, yes I did. You'll never guess how much." He lifted her in his arms and carried her to the easy chair. Sitting down, he laid her in his lap and threw the shawl over her shoulders. "When I first saw that painting, I was utterly stricken," he said softly, smoothing back a lock of her hair. "I wanted to touch the silk of the shawl, the folds of the dress, the girl's cheeks. I'd never been so drawn to a painting, or to a woman's face. If at that moment a genie had appeared and given me one wish, I would have wished for the girl to be real. And then I turned about and saw you!"

She couldn't quite believe it. "Are you saying you loved me *then?*"

"From that moment till time's end," he said.

"Oh, Harry, no," she laughed, trying to keep him from noticing her eyes tearing up. "Till time's end, indeed!"

"I think you'll discover, my love, that I, like you, don't easily change my mind."

Overwhelmed, she buried her face in his shoulder. She tried to tell him her feelings, but he was kissing her again. She let herself respond to the pressure of his embrace. The words would wait.

The library door opened silently, just wide enough for Leonard to peep in. When he saw that his friend was embracing Kate with such fervor that it was apparent even beneath the Persian shawl, he smiled, backed away, and carefully closed the door. But he didn't do it quickly enough to prevent Deirdre from getting a glimpse of the scene. "I declare!" she cried in horror. "Wasn't that Harry kissing *Kate?*"

"Might have been," Leonard said.

"Why, the bounder! It's only been a day since I jilted him. He's a more capricious, faithless rattlepate than I am."

Leonard was too wise to disagree. "Perhaps he is," he said, and led her away.

Elizabeth Mansfield

"Elizabeth Mansfield is renowned for delighting readers with deliciously different Regency romances." —Affaire de Coeur

"One of the enduring names in romance."
—The Paperback Forum